GREEK MYTHS

DK

CONTENTS

HEROES

ABOUT THE MYTHS

INTRODUCTION

The ancient Greek civilization stretched across the Mediterranean, but all parts shared many of the same gods and heroes. The stories about these figures are the Greek myths. Myths were how the ancient Greeks understood the world around them. They painted them on tableware, performed them in theatres, and even referenced them in courts of law. It is impossible to understand the ancient Greeks without understanding their myths and what these stories meant to them.

This was something I found out very quickly when I started learning about ancient Greece. But luckily for me, and you, the way that the ancient Greeks included myths in every part of their lives ensured that these stories would survive for thousands of years. By sharing them here, together, we are carrying on that tradition.

JEAN MENZIES, AUTHOR

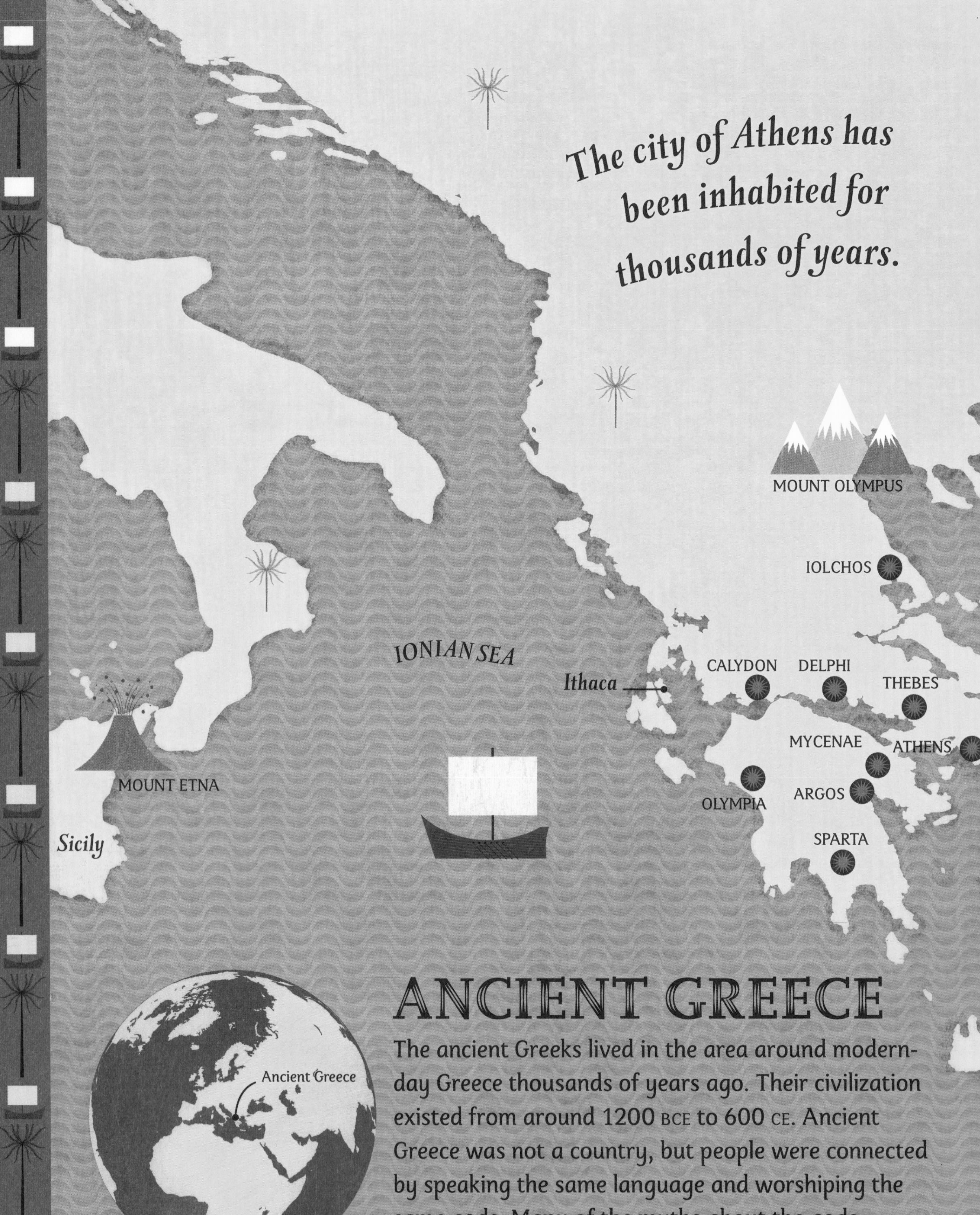

ANCIENT GREECE

The ancient Greeks lived in the area around modern-day Greece thousands of years ago. Their civilization existed from around 1200 BCE to 600 CE. Ancient Greece was not a country, but people were connected by speaking the same language and worshiping the same gods. Many of the myths about the gods happen in the cities and islands of ancient Greece.

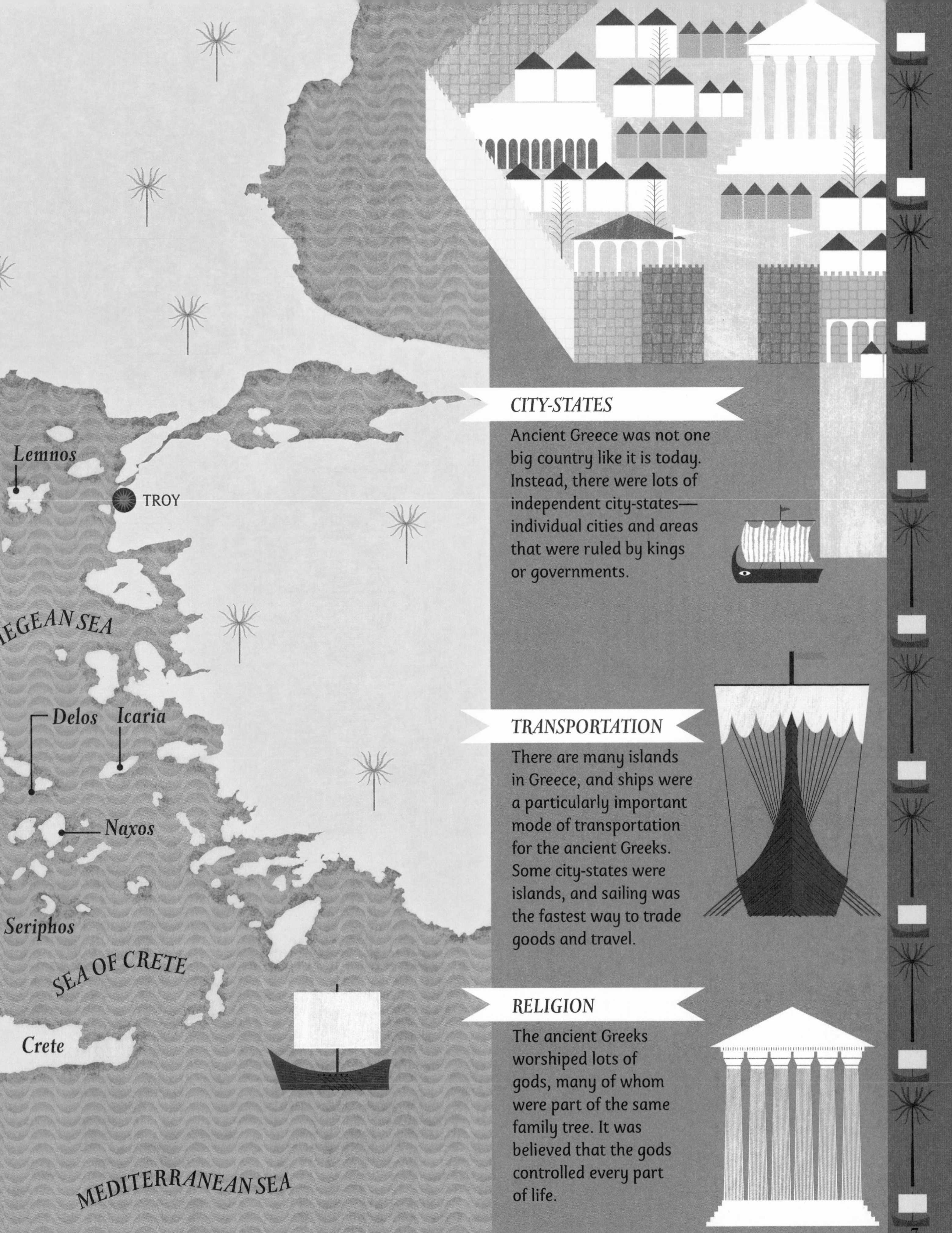

CITY-STATES

Ancient Greece was not one big country like it is today. Instead, there were lots of independent city-states—individual cities and areas that were ruled by kings or governments.

TRANSPORTATION

There are many islands in Greece, and ships were a particularly important mode of transportation for the ancient Greeks. Some city-states were islands, and sailing was the fastest way to trade goods and travel.

RELIGION

The ancient Greeks worshiped lots of gods, many of whom were part of the same family tree. It was believed that the gods controlled every part of life.

THE BEGINNING

To the ancient Greeks, myths were the same as history—they believed that all of the fantastical events in them had really happened once upon a time. The myths were their way of making sense of the past, even as far back as how the world was created.

These are the stories of the very first gods and goddesses, the mystical beings who forged the Earth and set rules for all others to follow.

The Creation

Life began with Chaos. This was the great chasm that was the universe. Chaos appeared with a massive yawn, and suddenly everything else came into being.

The first and most powerful of all the gods to spring from Chaos was Gaia—the Earth. Alone, she created the spiraling mountains where the rest of the gods would eventually live, as well as the sparkling sea, which lay over the land. She also made the god Ouranos, or the heavens, to rest above her.

Next to appear from Chaos after Gaia was Tartarus, the underworld, and Eros, or love. Finally, Chaos created Erebus, or darkness, and Nyx, the night. Together, Erebos and Nyx created Aether, or brightness, and Hemera, the day. These were the first gods.

Gaia was clothed in mountains and oceans.

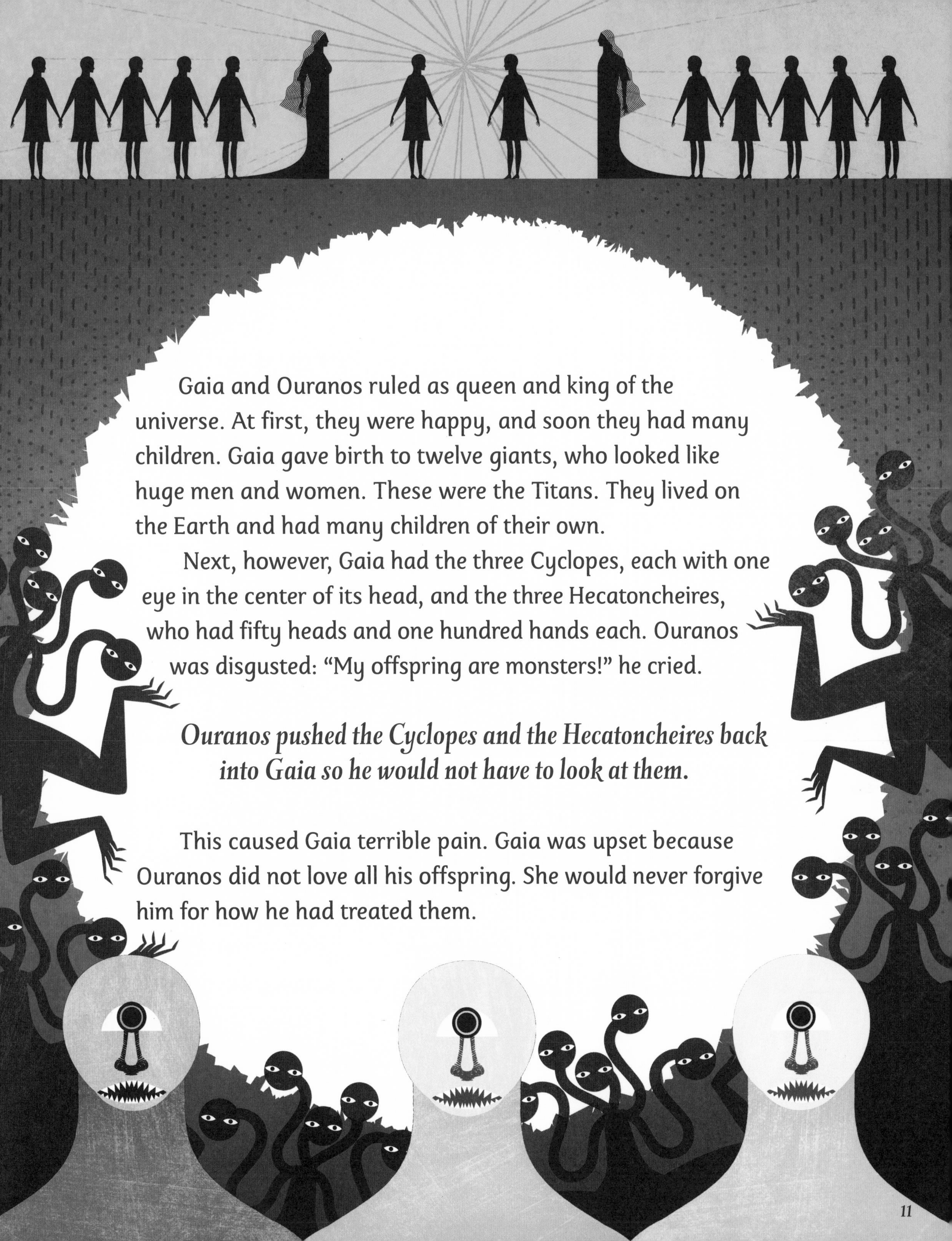

Gaia and Ouranos ruled as queen and king of the universe. At first, they were happy, and soon they had many children. Gaia gave birth to twelve giants, who looked like huge men and women. These were the Titans. They lived on the Earth and had many children of their own.

Next, however, Gaia had the three Cyclopes, each with one eye in the center of its head, and the three Hecatoncheires, who had fifty heads and one hundred hands each. Ouranos was disgusted: "My offspring are monsters!" he cried.

Ouranos pushed the Cyclopes and the Hecatoncheires back into Gaia so he would not have to look at them.

This caused Gaia terrible pain. Gaia was upset because Ouranos did not love all his offspring. She would never forgive him for how he had treated them.

The Fall of Ouranos

Unknown to Ouranos, Gaia had been harboring a great deal of anger toward him for banishing their children, the Hecatoncheires and the Cyclopes.

"Ouranos's power has gone to his head," Gaia thought. "Something needs to be done about it." She could not defeat Ouranos alone, because he could use his weight to overpower her. Instead, she went to her bravest son for help. This was the Titan named Cronos.

Cronos agreed to help Gaia conquer Ouranos if he could then rule the universe.

Gaia sharpened a piece of rock and used it to create a jagged-edged sickle, which she took to Cronos. "My son," she said, "take this sickle and wait here until your father, Ouranos, comes to visit me. Hide nearby, and when his back is turned, strike him!" Cronos, excited to have his father's power, grabbed it.

As Gaia had asked, Cronos waited until Ouranos appeared. Ouranos did not notice his son lying in wait. When Ouranos turned away, Cronos jumped out at his father and cut him with the sickle.

Gaia handed Cronos a sharp sickle.

"AHHH!" Ouranos screamed, but he could do nothing to fight back because he was in so much pain. From his wound, Ouranos's blood spilled into the sea and onto the ground. The blood that had fallen into the waves mixed with the salty water and began to foam. Gaia and Cronos watched as from the foam rose a giant scallop shell, which glided to the shore.

The scallop shell opened to reveal a beautiful woman—this was Aphrodite, the goddess of love.

Meanwhile, the blood that had landed on the ground had given rise to three terrifying winged women. Their names were Megaera, Tisiphone, and Alecto. Together, they were known as the Furies, goddesses of revenge. They would punish men and women who committed murder by driving them mad.

Ouranos fled back to the heavens and gave up his rule over the universe to his son, Cronos. Gaia was overjoyed—her other children could now be freed.

The Furies sprang from the blood that fell on the ground.

The Birth of Zeus

Once Cronos had defeated his father, Ouranos, he became king of the gods. He took his Titan sister Rhea to be his wife and queen.

First, to honor his promise to his mother, Gaia, he sent his brother Oceanus to release their gigantic siblings, the Hecatoncheires and the Cyclopes, from inside Gaia, where Ouranos had sent them. When they were brought to him, however, Cronos was threatened by their power and immediately sent them back. This infuriated Gaia, who cursed him: "Cronos, one day your own child will overthrow you, just as you overthrew your father."

Cronos was afraid of his mother's curse, so he decided to get rid of his children when they were babies.

Rhea and Cronos had six children. First, Rhea gave birth to three daughters—Hestia, Demeter, and Hera—and then two sons—Hades and Poseidon. One by one, as soon as they were born, Cronos took them from his wife and swallowed them whole. As immortal beings, they could not be killed, but all five children were trapped inside their father's stomach, unable to escape. Cronos was pleased with himself. "There's no way that Gaia's curse can come true now," he thought.

When Rhea became pregnant with her sixth child, she decided to try to protect her baby from Cronos. She traveled to Crete to give birth far away from her husband and asked her mother, Gaia, for help. Gaia assisted Rhea in delivering the boy and then hid him in a cave. When Cronos learned that Rhea had brought a son into the world, he went to find her and demanded: "Give me the boy!"

"Here you are," said Rhea. However, instead of giving Cronos his son to swallow, Rhea handed him a rock wrapped in a blanket. It did not even occur to Cronos to check what was inside.

Cronos swallowed the thickly swaddled rock without a second thought.

Rhea's youngest son was safe, and she named him Zeus. Since Cronos believed he had swallowed all six of his children, Zeus was able to grow up in peace.

Rhea entrusted Zeus to the care of Gaia, who looked after him until he reached adulthood. When Zeus was fully grown, he decided to try and free his brothers and sisters. He approached Metis, goddess of advice. “Can you help me free my siblings from the stomach of Cronos?” Zeus asked.

“I can brew a potion for you that will make Cronos sick, if you can slip it into his drink,” Metis offered.

Zeus took the potion from Metis, and set about planning how to trick his father into drinking it.

With the help of his mother, Rhea, Zeus sneaked into Cronos’s palace dressed as the cupbearer who served drinks to the gods. Never having seen his youngest son, Cronos did not recognize Zeus. He happily drank the wine Zeus poured for him, unaware that it had been mixed with Metis’s potion.

After only a few sips, Cronos turned pale. His stomach churned and his head began to spin, then “BLEURGH!” Cronos vomited up the swaddled stone, quickly followed by Poseidon, Hades, Hera, Demeter, and Hestia, now all fully grown. Zeus had freed them at last from their gruesome prison.

Cronos heaved and all the children he had swallowed emerged.

The War of the Titans

Zeus was angry at Cronos, his father. Cronos had swallowed Zeus's siblings and tried to keep them prisoner inside his stomach, so Zeus decided to challenge Cronos for control of the universe.

Cronos was not alone, however. Most of the Titans, Cronos's brothers and sisters, sided with him because they did not wish to be ruled by a younger god. Zeus's siblings also wanted revenge on Cronos, though. They were grateful to Zeus for rescuing them from Cronos's belly and they joined him to wage war against the Titans.

Both the Titans and the new gods were incredibly powerful.

However, the two sides were evenly matched in strength. They fought for 10 years, and still there was no end in sight. It was Gaia who gave her grandson Zeus a way to win the war. "Set my younger children free from their prison," she said. "The Cyclopes and Hecatoncheires remember how their brother Cronos betrayed them. They will join you in battle and help you defeat him."

Zeus dodged Kampe's stinging tail.

Zeus took his grandmother's advice and went down into the depths of the Earth to find his colossal relatives. They were guarded by the horrific monster Kampe, who had the head of a woman and the body of a deadly scorpion. Zeus darted this way and that to avoid Kampe's stinging tail. Finally, he lunged forward with his sword and CRUNCH! He pierced Kampe's tough shell, and the beast fell to the ground.

Thanks to Zeus, the Hecatoncheires and Cyclopes were free at last.

The Cyclopes, who were skilled in craftsmanship, were so grateful that they made gifts for Zeus and his brothers. To Hades, they gave a helmet of invisibility so he could sneak around unseen, and to Poseidon they gave a trident that could make the ground shake beneath him. As for Zeus himself, he was given thunderbolts to use as weapons.

Armed with their gifts from the Cyclopes, and joined by the one-hundred-handed Hecatoncheires, Zeus and the young gods launched a final attack on Cronos and the other Titans.

Swords clashed and thunderbolts flew, but eventually Zeus emerged triumphant.

Cronos and the Titans were defeated. To stop them from attacking the gods again, Zeus imprisoned them in the underworld. He commanded the Hecatoncheires to guard them to make sure that they never escaped.

Some of the Titans' children had joined their parents in opposing Zeus, including Atlas, who had led many of the Titan warriors. As a punishment, Zeus made him bear the weight of the heavens on his shoulders for the rest of time to keep them from falling down to Earth.

Meanwhile, those Titans who had fought on the side of Zeus were honored. The Titaness Styx had battled bravely, so Zeus commanded that all oaths made by the gods would be sworn on her name. From then on, she could punish any god who broke their promise.

Now the Titans were locked up deep underground, Zeus and the younger gods were the new rulers of the universe.

THE
OLYMPIAN
GODS

According to ancient Greek religion, there were many gods and goddesses, each responsible for a different part of everyday life. The most powerful of them, however, were the 12 Olympians.

It was the Olympians who the ancient Greeks worshiped with the largest temples and most lavish festivals. This was because these gods were in charge of the most essential aspects of life, from birth to death. They demanded respect.

Zeus, Hades, and Poseidon

The new generation of gods made their home on top of the tallest mountain in Greece—Mount Olympus.

Now that the Olympian gods were in charge, the time had come to divide up the world and decide who would rule its different parts. Although Zeus had led the fight against Cronos, he decided that it would be fair to share control over the Earth with his elder brothers, Hades and Poseidon. He gathered them together on Olympus.

Zeus, Poseidon, and Hades decided to draw lots to see who would rule which part of the world.

Three pebbles of different colors were selected, each one representing a different place. He who chose the white pebble would be king of the gods, he who chose the gray pebble would be god of the oceans, and he who chose the black pebble would be god of the underworld.

The gods drew lots to decide which part of the world they would rule.

The three pebbles were shaken in a helmet and Zeus was the first to choose. He closed his eyes and drew out the white pebble, so he got to rule over the heavens from the throne on Mount Olympus.

As their king, Zeus became the most powerful of all the gods.

Poseidon was next, and he drew out the gray pebble. This meant that he would rule the vast sparkling seas that covered the Earth's surface and have control over all of the creatures that lived in them.

Hades was the last brother to choose, and he was left with the black pebble. The only part of the world that was left was the underworld deep below the ground, where the souls of men and women were sent after death.

Every role was an important one, however, and each god accepted his new kingdom graciously.

The Sun, the Moon, and the Dawn

Helios and Selene were brother and sister, the god of the sun and the goddess of the moon. Eos was the goddess of the dawn, who turned the sky rosy each morning.

EOS FALLS IN LOVE

Every morning, Eos created the dawn and opened the gates of Olympus, so Helios could ride his sun chariot out into the sky.

From the gates, Eos looked down on the Earth, and the kingdom of Troy in particular, where the prince Tithonos lived. Eos was in love with Tithonos. One day, she decided to travel down to Troy to meet him.

Tithonos fell in love with Eos, too, so they married. However, Tithonos was a mortal, which meant that one day he would die. Determined never to be parted from him, Eos went to Zeus. “Please, Zeus, grant Tithonos immortality,” she begged.

Zeus did as Eos asked, but she had forgotten an important part—to ask for Tithonos to have eternal youth. So, although he lived forever, he continued to age, growing ever older and weaker.

Eos pushed open the gates to Olympus each morning.

HELIOS AND PHAËTHON

Helios rode his chariot across the sky each day, pulling the burning sun behind him.

Now, Helios had a young son named Phaëthon, but Phaëthon refused to believe that he was the son of a god. One day he demanded of Helios: "If you really are my father, then let me drive your chariot today."

Helios doubted that Phaëthon would be able to command the willful horses, but he could not say no to his son. He placed the boy in the chariot and handed him the reins. Sure enough, Phaëthon quickly lost control and began to careen across the sky, threatening to burn the Earth.

Zeus, who was watching from Mount Olympus, knew he had to act to save the world. He threw one of his thunderbolts and struck the boy, stopping the chariot, but killing Phaëthon.

SELENE SAVES OLYMPUS

Each night, as Helios returned to Olympus, Selene set out in her shining silver chariot to break up the darkness with the light of the moon.

Typhoeus was a monstrous giant. Hundreds of snakes grew from his shoulders and he flew with a huge pair of wings. He had decided to challenge Zeus for his throne, and one night he charged on Mount Olympus. Selene loved Zeus, so when the king of the gods was threatened, she rushed to his aid.

Selene saw Typhoeus and stood guard at the gates. He hurled ferocious bulls at Selene, but she did not back down. She batted away each bull and was able to beat Typhoeus back. From that day on, the white surface of the moon was scarred by dark spots, where she had been hit.

ZEUS

KING OF THE GODS

Zeus was the youngest of his siblings, but also the most powerful. He became king of the gods after overthrowing his father, Cronos. With his wife, Hera, Zeus ruled the heavens from Mount Olympus. He threw powerful thunderbolts at anyone who angered him.

PARENTS: Cronos and Rhea

CHILDREN: Apollo, Ares, Artemis, Athena, Dionysus, Helen, Herakles, Hermes, Minos, Persephone, Perseus, and many more

SACRED SYMBOLS

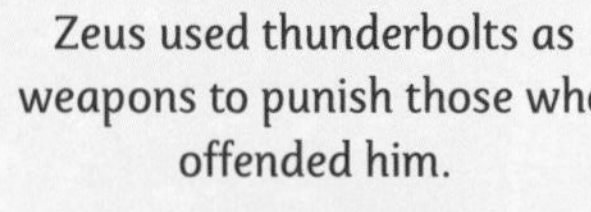

THUNDERBOLT
Zeus used thunderbolts as weapons to punish those who offended him.

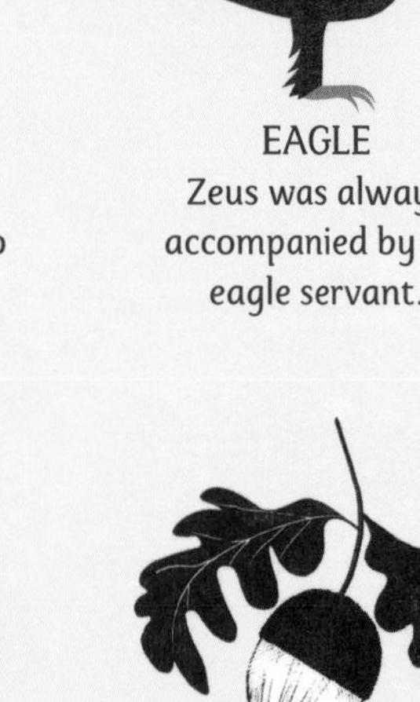

EAGLE
Zeus was always accompanied by his eagle servant.

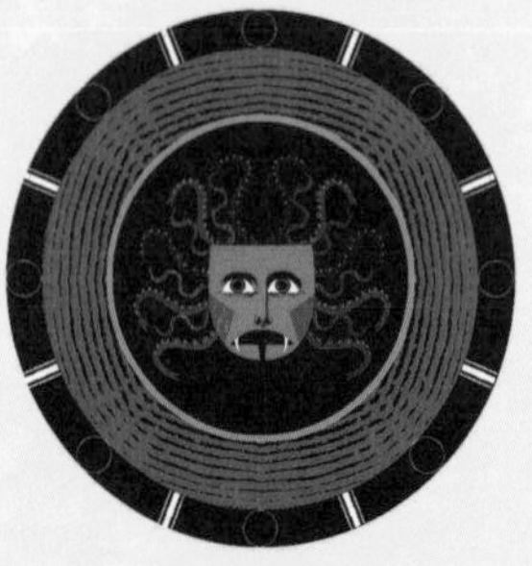

AEGIS
The aegis was a shield made by Hephaestus. It had the face of Medusa on it.

OAK TREE
The oak was Zeus's sacred tree, and he could speak to his worshipers from oak trees.

JUDGE AND JURY

Zeus enforced the law among the gods, and the ancient Greeks often made promises in front of statues of him. In Olympia, where the Olympic Games were first held, athletes swore an oath to Zeus that they would not cheat.

HERA

QUEEN OF THE GODS

Hera was the eldest child of Rhea and Cronos. She married her brother Zeus and became queen of the gods, ruling with him on Mount Olympus. Hera was extremely jealous of any other god or human that Zeus loved, and she often punished them horribly.

PARENTS: Cronos and Rhea

CHILDREN: Ares, Hephaestus, and many more

SACRED SYMBOLS

LOTUS
Hera often carried a staff with a lotus flower on the end.

CROWN
As queen of the Olympian gods, Hera always wore a crown.

COW
Hera turned the mortal Io into a cow out of jealousy when Io had children with Zeus.

PEACOCK
Hera made peacocks when her servant Argos died, and she moved his hundred eyes to the bird's feathers.

PROTECTOR OF WOMEN

As Zeus's wife and queen of the gods, Hera was worshiped as the goddess of marriage and family. Women in particular would pray to Hera in temples and at home, asking for her blessing on their marriage.

Apollo and Artemis

Once he took the throne on Mount Olympus, Zeus married his sister Hera. Together, they had many children, including Ares, the god of war.

However, even though Zeus was married to Hera, he continued to fall in love with other goddesses and mortal women, and he fathered many more children. Some of these children were born as gods, too, and this made Hera extremely jealous.

In her anger, Hera often punished the women Zeus loved, whoever they were.

Hera seethed with jealousy.

Leto was goddess of motherhood and Zeus thought she was very beautiful. They fell in love and Leto became pregnant with twins.

When Hera discovered Leto was pregnant, she was furious. Terrified of what Hera might do, Leto fled and tried to find a new home where Hera would not find her. No one would take her in, however, out of fear of Hera. The only place that Leto was able to find safety was on the floating island of Delos.

The island had never settled in one place. Instead, it drifted over the blue waves of the Aegean Sea.

When Leto set foot on Delos though, the island stood still. Four huge columns appeared that anchored it to the seabed.

There, Leto gave birth first to a daughter, whom she named Artemis. For nine long days, Leto struggled to give birth to her second child. In the end, Artemis—who had grown quickly—helped her mother deliver the baby, named Apollo. Both Artemis and Apollo were gods. Artemis became the goddess of hunting and Apollo the god of music. Eventually, Hera forgot her anger toward Leto and they all went to live on Mount Olympus.

The Birth of Athena

Metis, the goddess of advice, had helped Zeus free his siblings from the stomach of his father, Cronos. She was also very beautiful, and Zeus had fallen in love with her.

Metis, however, did not feel the same way about Zeus. She tried to avoid him by transforming into various different animals—first a bird, then a lion, then a deer, and so on. Zeus eventually caught up with her when she was in her human form, however. Soon Metis became pregnant.

Meanwhile, Gaia, goddess of the Earth, had made a prophecy that any son born to Metis would one day overthrow Zeus, just as he had overthrown Cronos before him. This worried Zeus.

Inspired by his father, Zeus decided to swallow Metis whole, along with their unborn baby.

"This way," Zeus thought smugly, "Gaia's prophecy can't possibly come true."

Nine months later, however, Zeus was struck by a headache so strong that it felt as if the Cyclopes themselves were hammering at his skull.

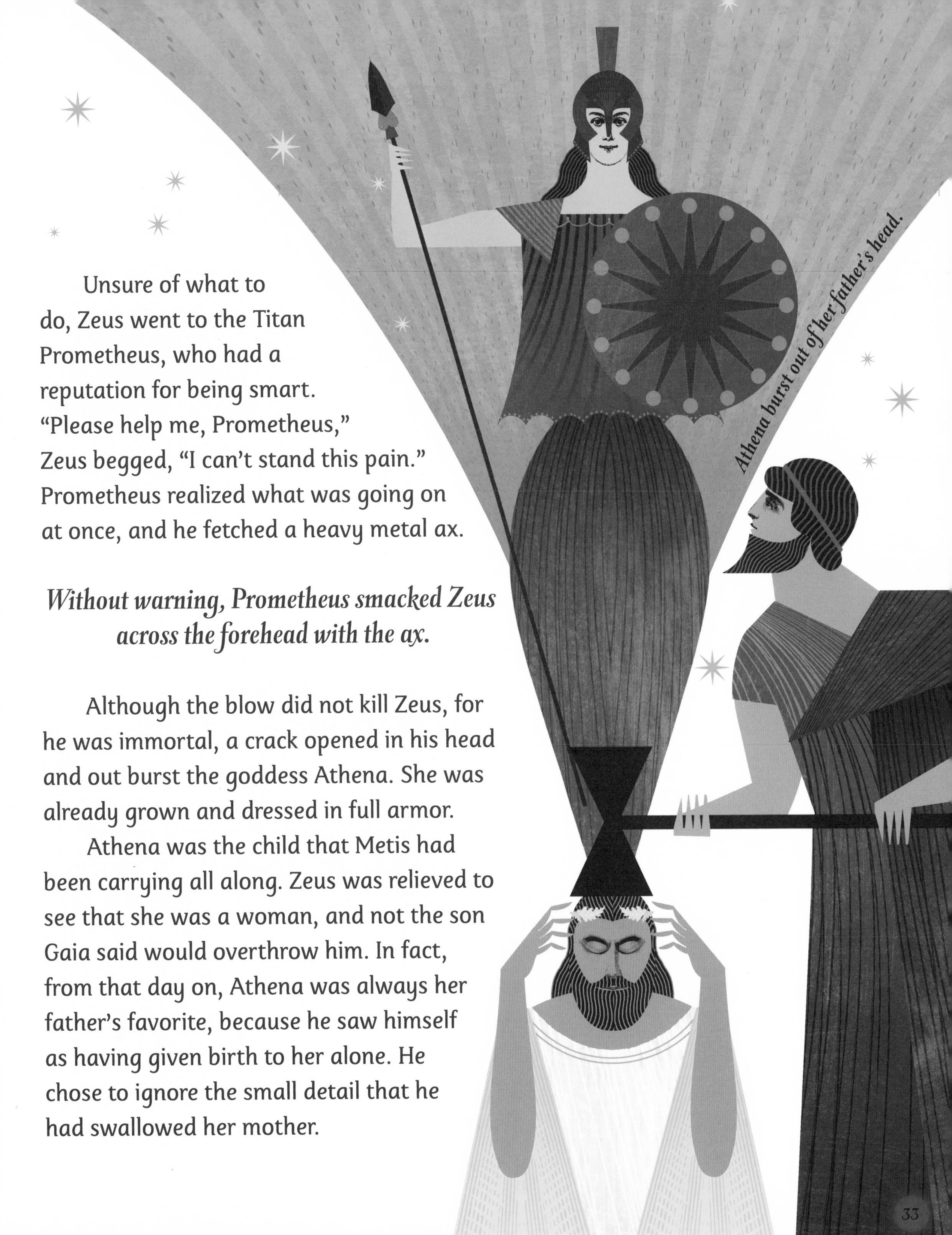

Unsure of what to do, Zeus went to the Titan Prometheus, who had a reputation for being smart. "Please help me, Prometheus," Zeus begged, "I can't stand this pain." Prometheus realized what was going on at once, and he fetched a heavy metal ax.

Without warning, Prometheus smacked Zeus across the forehead with the ax.

Although the blow did not kill Zeus, for he was immortal, a crack opened in his head and out burst the goddess Athena. She was already grown and dressed in full armor.

Athena was the child that Metis had been carrying all along. Zeus was relieved to see that she was a woman, and not the son Gaia said would overthrow him. In fact, from that day on, Athena was always her father's favorite, because he saw himself as having given birth to her alone. He chose to ignore the small detail that he had swallowed her mother.

Athena burst out of her father's head.

The Birth of Dionysus

Semele was a priestess at a temple dedicated to Zeus. One day, after she had sacrificed a bull to the god, she went out swimming to wash off the blood.

Zeus happened to be flying overhead in the shape of an eagle, and when he spotted Semele, he immediately fell madly in love. He changed into a mortal shape to speak to her.

Semele was very pleased to have the attention of the god she had worshiped for so many years.

When Semele learned she was pregnant with Zeus's child, she was overjoyed, as was Zeus. "Dearest Semele," he said, "I love you so much. I swear on the Styx River that you can ask me for anything and I will give it to you."

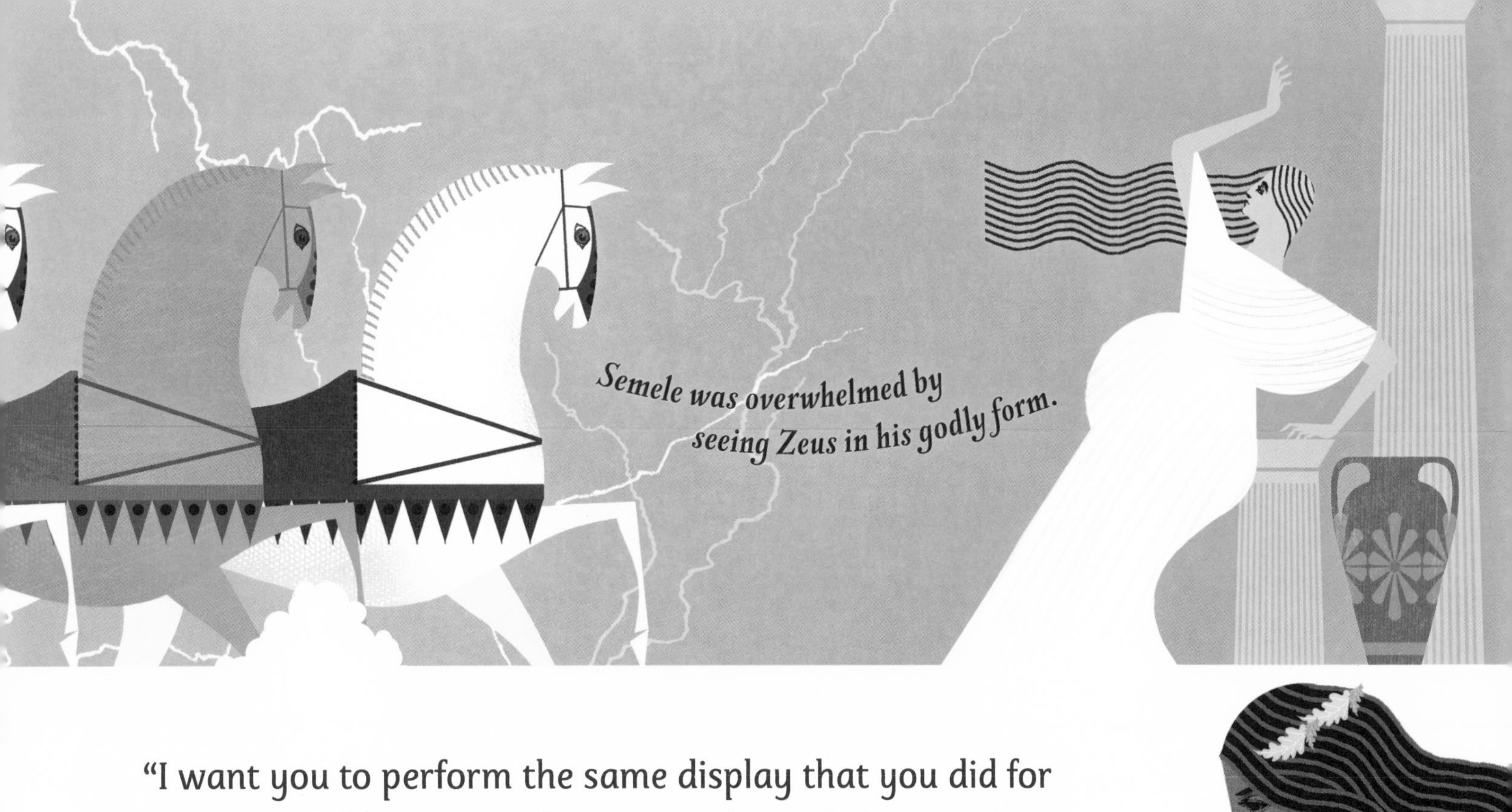

Semele was overwhelmed by seeing Zeus in his godly form.

"I want you to perform the same display that you did for Hera at your wedding," Semele requested, "and show me how you look in your godly form." Zeus was dismayed, because he knew what would happen to Semele if he did what she asked, but, bound by the oath he had made, he agreed.

The next night, Zeus appeared to Semele riding in an ornate chariot, surrounded by clouds of crashing thunder and flashes of blinding lightning.

The violent noises startled Semele, and when she gazed upon Zeus approaching in all his shining glory, the sight was so terrifying that instantly she died of fright. Although Zeus was unable to save Semele, he did manage to rescue the baby from her body. The tiny boy was not yet ready to be born, however, so Zeus sewed him into a cut that he made in his thigh. When the infant was ready, Zeus removed him from his leg and named him Dionysus. A new god was born.

Zeus gave birth to Dionysus from his leg.

Hermes and the Lyre

Maia was an ocean nymph, daughter of the Titans Atlas and Pleione. Together, she and Zeus had a son named Hermes.

Hermes was a particularly mischievous child. In fact, he grew up to be the god of tricksters. One day, he escaped from Maia and decided to steal a herd of prized cows from his half brother, the god Apollo.

So that Apollo could not find the cows, Hermes cast a spell on them so that they could only walk backward.

When Apollo found his field empty of cattle, he went to look at their hoofprints, but he could not figure out where they had gone. The prints led into the field, but his cows were nowhere to be seen.

While Apollo was puzzling over his missing cattle, Hermes had sacrificed one of the cows to the older gods and cut up its body into pieces. When he was looking at its intestines, he was struck by an

Hermes enchanted the cows to walk backward.

ingenious idea. Hermes cut up the intestines and then located a tortoise shell. He strung the guts across it and plucked them as strings. Clear notes rang out!

Hermes had crafted the first lyre.

Eventually, Apollo discovered Hermes with his cows. He was furious. “How dare you kill one of my prize cows!” Apollo roared.

Thinking quickly, Hermes held up the lyre he had made. “I’m sorry, Apollo,” Hermes said. “Please take this instrument in return for your cow.”

When Apollo played the lyre, the sound it produced was so beautiful the flowers and trees swayed along to the music. Apollo felt this gift was a fair trade for his cow, and he forgave Hermes. From that day on, Apollo was rarely without his tuneful lyre.

Hephaestus's Revenge

Hera was jealous of Zeus's many children, so, being a goddess, she decided to give birth to a son by herself. This child was hers alone, and she named him Hephaestus.

Equally as capable of jealousy as his wife, Zeus disliked Hephaestus from the start. One evening, Zeus became so angry that he threw the boy from Mount Olympus with all his might. Mount Olympus was so tall and Zeus flung him so far that Hephaestus fell for an entire day. He fell and fell, rushing past clouds and birds, before finally landing on the Greek island of Lemnos.

When Hephaestus hit the ground, the bones in his foot shattered and he would always walk with a limp. Luckily, he was spotted by the Sintians, a group of clever pirates. They took in Hephaestus and looked after him. They also trained him to be a smith, and Hephaestus discovered that he was gifted with great skill in crafting metals.

Hephaestus could shape anything from iron, silver, bronze, or gold. He became the god of smiths.

Hephaestus decided to use his new skills to reclaim a place on Mount Olympus. He set about making a spectacular gold throne that was studded with precious stones. He gave it to his mother, Hera, as a gift. Hera admired the finely crafted chair and sat down on it immediately, but she had been tricked. The throne had a spell on it! Golden chains appeared and fastened around her arms and legs.

Hera was trapped, unable to get up from her throne.

Zeus was furious. "Release Hera immediately," he thundered at Hephaestus.

"Not until you show me the respect I deserve as a god," Hephaestus replied.

Zeus thought about this for a moment. "All right, Hephaestus," he said. "If you release your mother, then I will let you return to Mount Olympus and marry Aphrodite."

Aphrodite was the goddess of beauty, and Hephaestus agreed at once. From that day on, he lived on Mount Olympus with the gods.

Hera was bound to the throne by golden chains.

DEMETER

GODDESS OF THE HARVEST

Demeter was responsible for making sure the crops grew and that the land was fertile. She preferred to live on Earth with her daughter, Persephone, than on Mount Olympus with the other gods, including Zeus, Persephone's father. When she was unhappy, plants would wither and die.

PARENTS: Cronos and Rhea

CHILDREN: Persephone and many more

SACRED SYMBOLS

CORNUCOPIA
This was a large goat's horn that provided an endless supply of food.

TORCH
Demeter was often shown with two fiery crossed torches.

SNAKE
Demeter's chariot was drawn by two massive snakes.

WHEAT
This crop was grown to make flour and bread. Demeter often held a sheaf of wheat.

SECRET CEREMONY

Demeter and Persephone were worshiped in a secret ceremony called the Eleusinian Mysteries. This event was held in the city of Eleusis and the only people who knew what was involved were those who made it through a series of tasks.

POSEIDON

GOD OF THE SEA

Poseidon was the middle brother, between Hades and Zeus. He was married to the nymph Amphitrite, who was responsible for helping him keep the sea calm. Together, they had one son, Triton, who was the first merman—a man with the tail of a fish.

PARENTS: Cronos and Rhea

CHILDREN: Bellerophon, Orion, Pegasus, Pelias, Polyphemus, Triton, and many more

SACRED SYMBOLS

HORSE
Poseidon was god of horses and he often disguised himself as one.

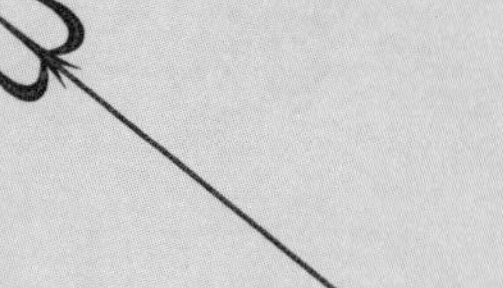

TRIDENT
This was a three-pronged spear Poseidon used to wield his power.

DOLPHIN
As god of the sea, Poseidon was often accompanied by one or more dolphins.

EARTHQUAKE
Poseidon could cause earthquakes by hitting the ground with his trident.

STORM-BRINGER

Because Poseidon ruled over the sea, sailors prayed to him for protection, sometimes drowning animals as sacrifices. The ancient Greeks thought that he could whip up storms by wielding his trident.

The Kidnapping of Persephone

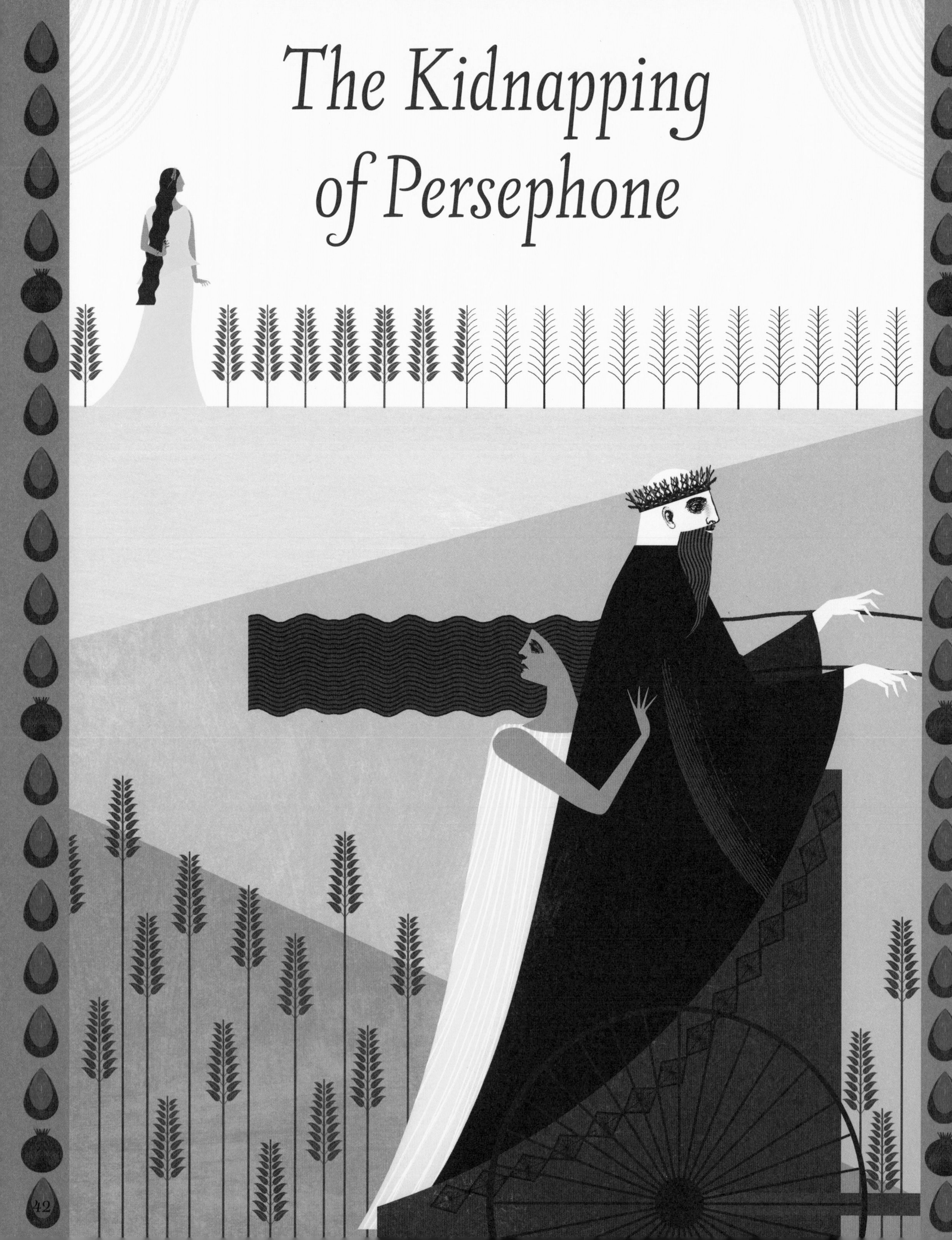

The volcano Mount Etna was rumbling.

Persephone was the daughter of proud Zeus, king of the gods, and kind Demeter, goddess of the harvest. She was a gentle girl, who lived with her mother on the island of Sicily.

There, she helped Demeter tend to the Earth and make plants grow. However, Sicily was also home to the great volcano Mount Etna. One afternoon, when Persephone was out walking in the countryside, the volcano began to rumble. Smoke streamed from its crater and powerful tremors caused the ground to crack wide open.

Persephone stumbled back from the fracture in the ground in surprise.

Hades saw what was happening from the underworld and raced to the surface in his chariot to inspect the fracture. "I must seal this new entrance to my kingdom," he thought, "but wait... who is that?" When he caught sight of the lovely Persephone, Hades fell in love instantly. "She must be my wife!" he decided. Seizing his chance, Hades rode by Persephone and pulled her into the chariot beside him. They went back through the opening, and the earth closed behind them. On the ground, it was as if nothing had happened.

When Persephone did not return home, Demeter was struck with fear. She searched all over the world, but couldn't find Persephone anywhere. Eventually, she went to speak to Helios, the sun god, who saw everything that happened on Earth. "Have you seen my daughter?" she asked, and he told her what had happened. Demeter was so overcome by sadness that she gave up caring for the Earth and making sure that the plants grew.

Soon, crops across the land began to die and the humans could not understand why.

Zeus saw what was happening and called on Demeter to explain. "Hades has kidnapped my daughter," Demeter told Zeus. "I won't make anything grow until she is returned."

Zeus did not want the humans to starve—without them, who would give sacrifices to the gods? "I will try to bring Persephone back to you," he promised Demeter, "but she cannot leave if she has eaten any food in the

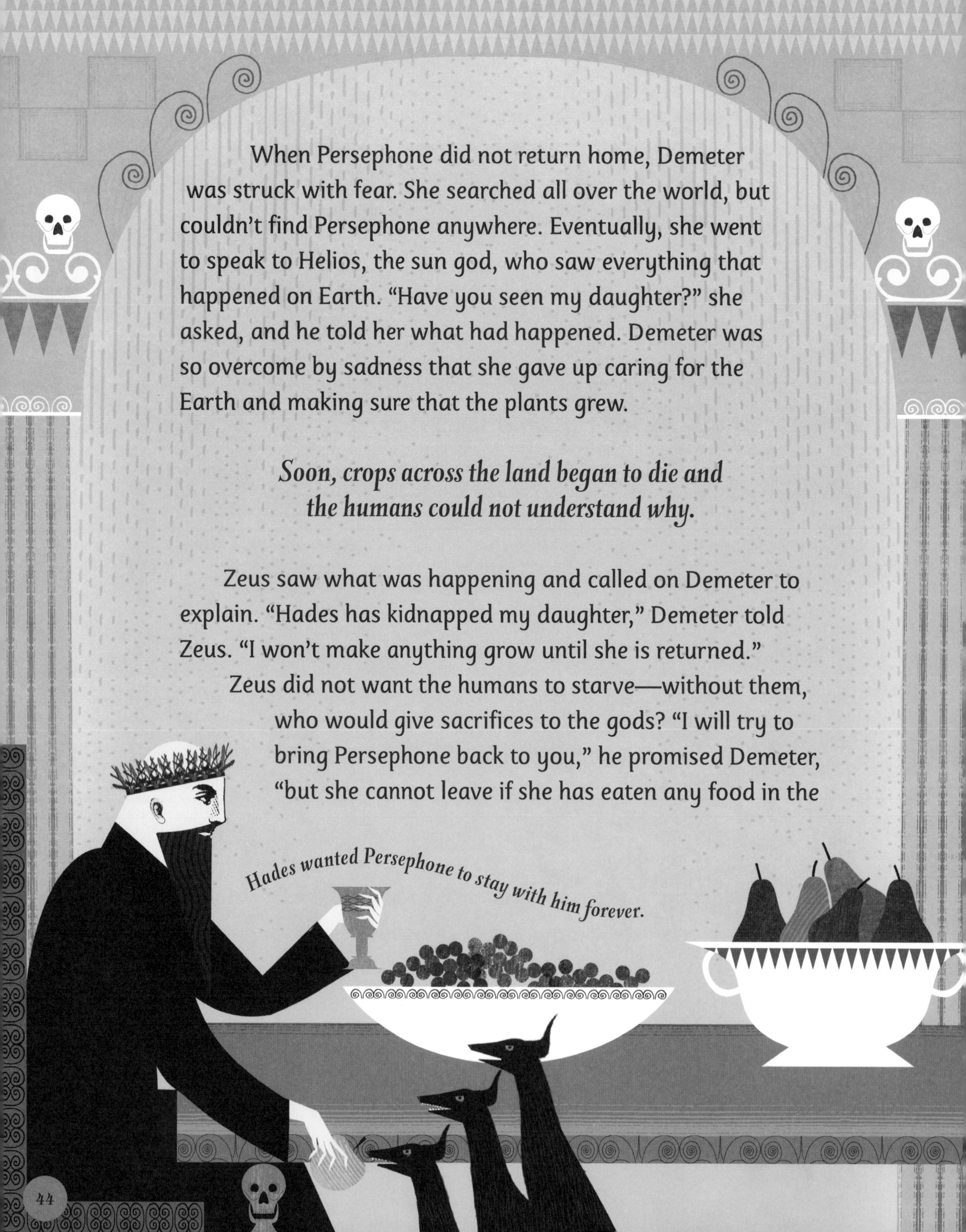

Hades wanted Persephone to stay with him forever.

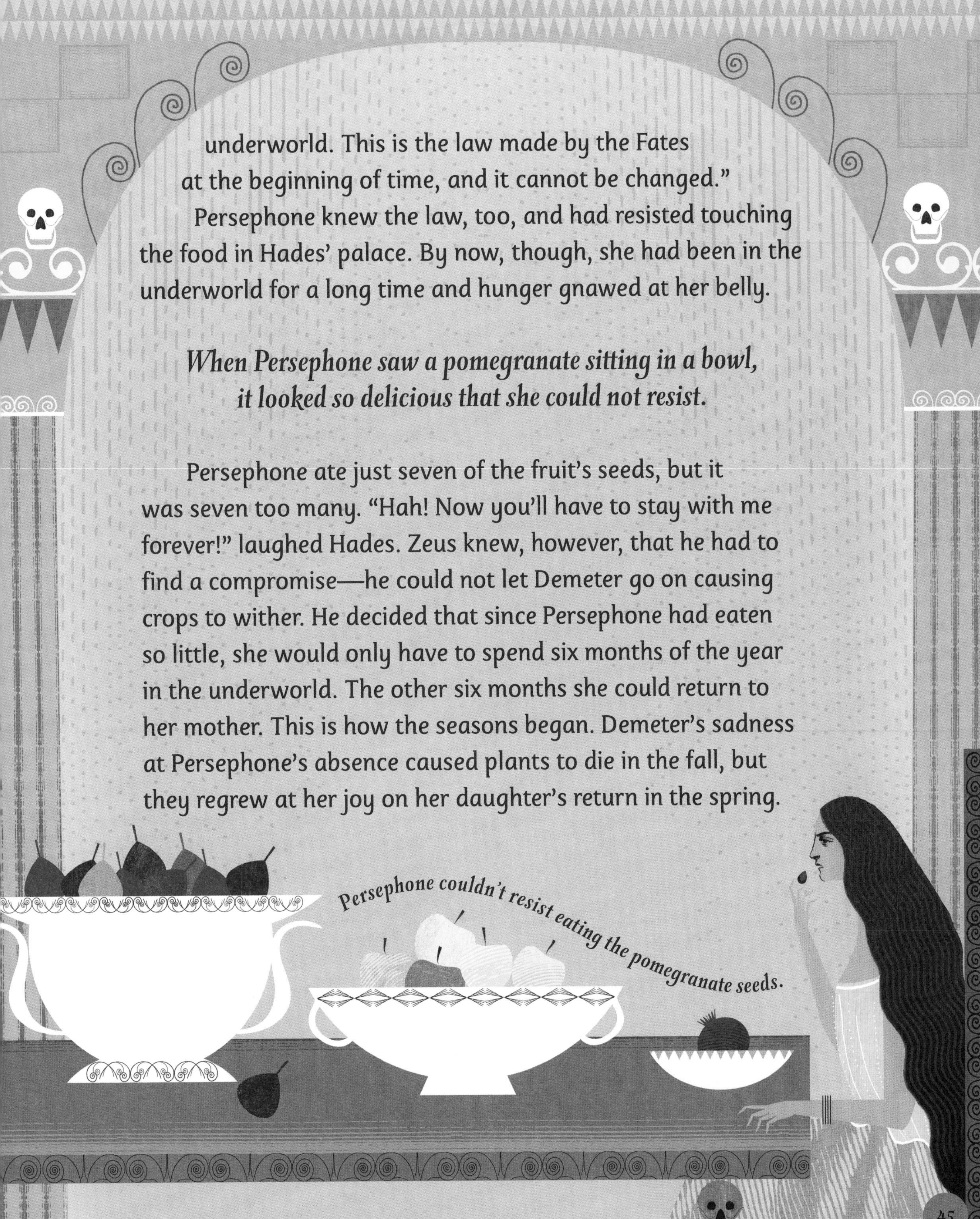

underworld. This is the law made by the Fates at the beginning of time, and it cannot be changed."

Persephone knew the law, too, and had resisted touching the food in Hades' palace. By now, though, she had been in the underworld for a long time and hunger gnawed at her belly.

When Persephone saw a pomegranate sitting in a bowl, it looked so delicious that she could not resist.

Persephone ate just seven of the fruit's seeds, but it was seven too many. "Hah! Now you'll have to stay with me forever!" laughed Hades. Zeus knew, however, that he had to find a compromise—he could not let Demeter go on causing crops to wither. He decided that since Persephone had eaten so little, she would only have to spend six months of the year in the underworld. The other six months she could return to her mother. This is how the seasons began. Demeter's sadness at Persephone's absence caused plants to die in the fall, but they regrew at her joy on her daughter's return in the spring.

Persephone couldn't resist eating the pomegranate seeds.

HADES

GOD OF THE UNDERWORLD

GOD

Hades was the eldest son of Cronos and Rhea. He was married to Persephone, who ruled at his side in the underworld. Although Hades kept the underworld running smoothly, he was not responsible for judging or punishing the dead. He did make sure no one left, though.

PARENTS: Cronos and Rhea

CHILDREN: Many

SACRED SYMBOLS

CYPRESS TREE
Hades was associated with the cypress tree, since it was the tree of mourning.

NARCISSUS
The narcissus was the flower that Persephone had stopped to pick when Hades first saw her.

KEY
The gates to the underworld were locked with a golden key.

CAP OF INVISIBILTY
Hades' helmet made the wearer invisible. It was given to him by the Cyclopes.

UNDERGROUND PRAYERS

Since Hades lived beneath the ground and could not easily see what was going on in the world above, his worshipers would thump their fists on the ground and cry out when they wanted to be heard by him.

DIONYSUS

GOD OF WINE

Dionysus was one of the youngest Olympian gods. He was married to the mortal woman Ariadne, whom he took from Theseus when they were sailing back after killing the Minotaur. Always fond of a celebration, he was responsible for parties and theater, in addition to being the god of wine.

PARENTS: Zeus and Semele

CHILDREN: Many

SACRED SYMBOLS

THEATER
Theater was invented to be performed in honor of Dionysus.

BULL
The bull was Dionysus's favored animal, and he often had bull's horns.

GRAPES
Grapes are used to make wine. Dionysus was often seen with vines or a wine cup.

IVY
Dionysus's mother, Semele, strung ivy in her hair when she was pregnant.

WOMEN WORSHIPERS

Dionysus's most dedicated followers were known as maenads. These were women who dedicated themselves to the worship of Dionysus through drinking and dancing. In some tales, they descended into madness during their celebrations.

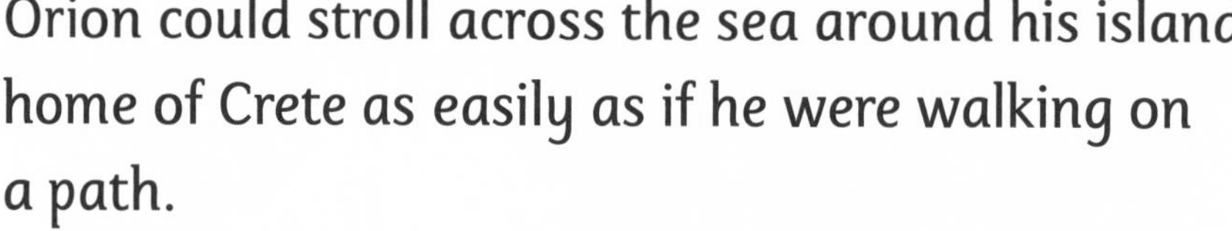

Orion

Orion was the son of Euryale, princess of Crete, and Poseidon, god of the sea. His powerful father had gifted him the ability to walk on water.

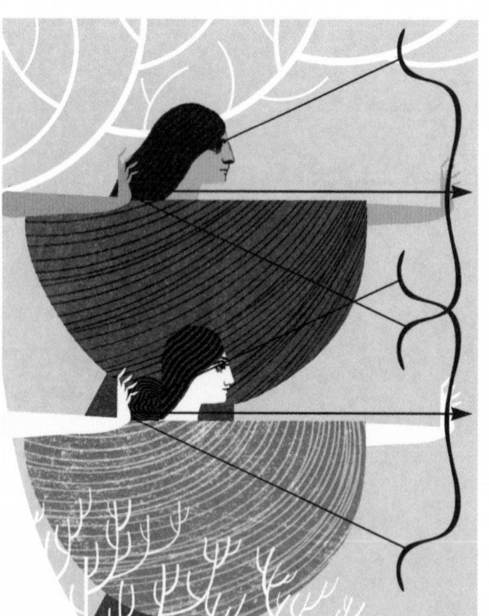

Orion could stroll across the sea around his island home of Crete as easily as if he were walking on a path.

He was also an impressive hunter, chasing animals over land and water. In addition to spirited wild goats and quick-footed hares, he could catch slippery fish, big and small. His talent for capturing prey made him a favorite of Artemis, goddess of hunting. The two would often spend all day together, running through the forests of Crete.

Orion and Artemis thought their time together would never end.

However, Orion became arrogant. One day, as he and Artemis stalked a hare, he boasted, "I bet I could catch and kill any animal that lives on the land." Artemis simply laughed.

Unfortunately for Orion, Artemis was not the only goddess to hear his claim. Gaia, goddess of the Earth, had been listening. His bragging outraged her. She decided to conjure up a cruel test for Orion.

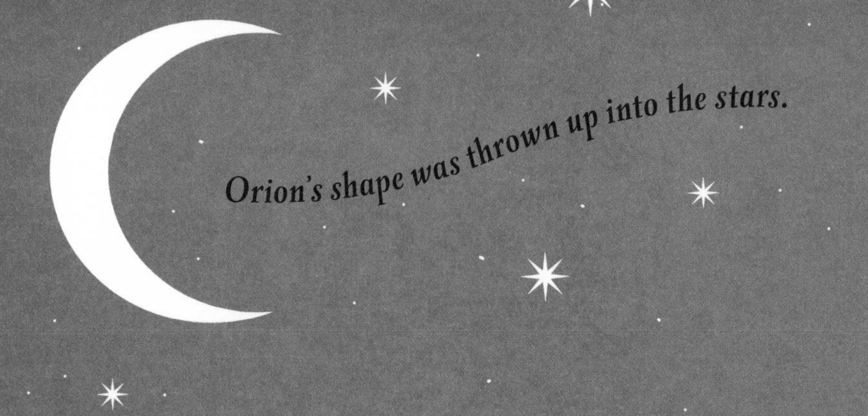

Orion's shape was thrown up into the stars.

From the dirt around his feet, she created the glinting black body of a huge scorpion.

Gaia breathed life into the creature, which scuttled toward Orion.

When Orion saw the terrible monster, he quickly drew his bow. He fired arrow after arrow, but they simply bounced off the creature's body. Its hard, armorlike shell could not be pierced. It snapped at Orion with its claws, driving him back. Finally, the scorpion jabbed at him with its venomous sting and Orion dropped down dead.

Artemis fell to the forest floor weeping. The goddess called to her father, Zeus, for help, but he could not bring Orion back to life. Instead, he sent the young man's soul up into the heavens. There, it split into tiny pieces that hung in the sky as stars so that no one would ever forget him. It is the constellation Orion.

Artemis went to her father, Zeus, for help.

HUMANS AND THE GODS

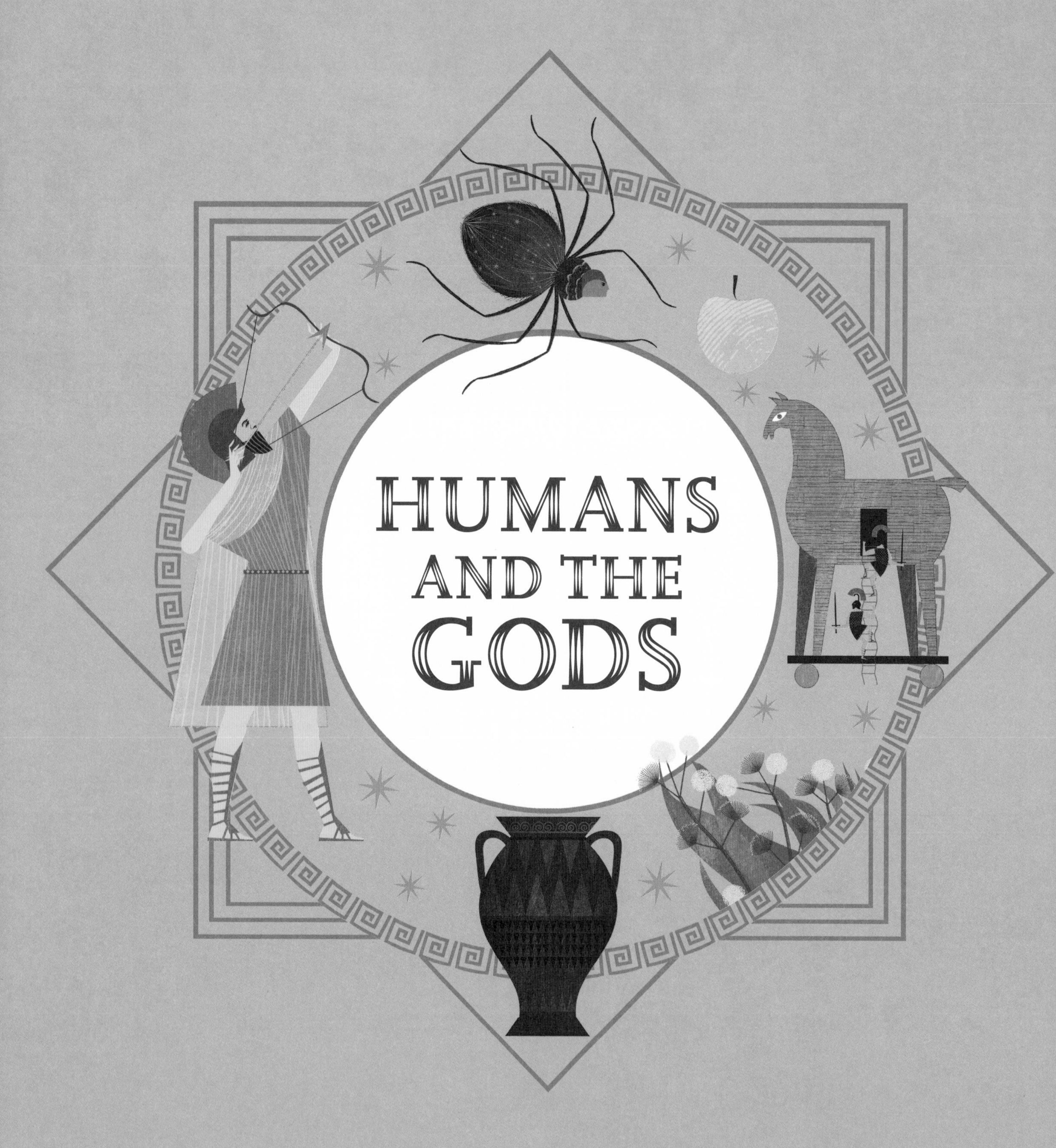

Once the Olympian gods ruled the world, they decided to populate it with humans. From the beginning, however, the humans and the gods had a difficult relationship.

Sometimes the gods were cruel, while other times they were generous. Still, people had to learn to live in a world where their gods were unpredictable—and they had to be careful to keep the gods happy. These are the stories of how they fared.

Prometheus sculpted men from mud.

Prometheus Makes Man

Prometheus and Epimetheus were two of the Titans not to be imprisoned by Zeus. They had fought on the side of the Olympians in the War of the Titans.

Epimetheus decided what every animal should be like.

For their help, Zeus gave them the important job of filling the Earth with life. Prometheus and Epimetheus created all the animals that ran and climbed, from the mightiest elephants to the tiniest ants.

Epimetheus named each species and decided whether it should be strong or fast, clever or dangerous.

Prometheus, however, spent most of his time creating something different—mortal men. He molded them out of water and earth, modeling them in the image of the gods themselves.

When they were done, Zeus looked at Prometheus's prized creations. "Prometheus, in exchange for their lives on Earth, these mortals must give regular gifts to the gods," he ordered.

Prometheus was a mischievous Titan, however. "I don't see why Zeus should have control over my creations," he thought to himself.

The furious Zeus found only bones inside the fat offered to him by the mortals.

Prometheus went to the mortals and said, "You are to sacrifice an ox to the king of the gods, Zeus. However, I want you to wrap the tastiest meat inside the stomach and I want you to disguise the bones in the delicious fat."

As Prometheus hoped, when the humans offered their gifts to Zeus, he chose the rich fat rather than the ox's stomach, unaware that the fat hid dry bones.

Zeus was outraged that Prometheus had tricked him out of the best part of the animal—but the damage was done. From that day on, mortals only gave the leftovers of sacrifices to the gods and kept the meat for themselves.

Zeus decided to ban men from having fire as a punishment.

Without fire, the mortals could not keep warm or cook. Prometheus thought this was unfair, however, so he sneaked a small flame from Olympus down to Earth hidden inside the stalk of a fennel plant and gave fire to the humans.

When Zeus discovered what Prometheus had done, he was furious. He ordered Prometheus to be chained to the Caucasos Mountains. Every day, Zeus sent an eagle to peck at Prometheus's stomach and eat his liver, while the Titan could do nothing. Because he was an immortal being, every night Prometheus would heal, and the punishment would start again the next day.

Prometheus endured this torture for many years, but he was eventually freed by Zeus's son, the hero Heracles.

Prometheus suffered the same punishment every day.

Pandora's Jar

Zeus had punished the Titan Prometheus for giving fire to humans, but he was also angry with mortal men for having fire when he had forbidden it.

Zeus went to Hephaestus, god of smiths and a master craftsman, to ask for help. "I want you to assist me in making a female mortal," said Zeus, "just as Prometheus made men." Together, the two gods gathered handfuls of soil and water and sculpted a beautiful lady—this was the first woman.

Zeus named her Pandora, which meant "all gifts."

Zeus next went to Athena. "I want you to dress this woman in fine silks and weave flowers through her hair," he ordered. Once Athena had dressed Pandora, Zeus placed a golden crown on Pandora's brow. It was forged by Hephaestus and made of golden models of all the animals of the world.

Zeus then gave Pandora to Epimetheus, Prometheus's brother, as a bride. Epimetheus did not think to question Zeus's gift and he accepted his new wife gladly.

Pandora accidentally unleashed all the evils of the world.

However, Zeus had also given Pandora a jar to take with her to Earth. As he handed it to her, he warned, "Pandora, you must never, ever, open this jar."

For some time, Epimetheus and Pandora lived together happily, but Pandora could not forget about the jar. "Why would Zeus give me something that I cannot open?" she thought. Finally, one day, Pandora was so overwhelmed by curiosity that she took the jar from its hiding place and pulled the stopper from the neck.

In that moment, everything evil swarmed out into the world.

The previously peaceful Earth was now flooded with plague, famine, and every type of disaster that Zeus had hidden in the jar.

All might have been lost if it were not for Pandora's quick reactions.

She immediately put the lid back on the jar and, although it was almost empty, she did manage to stop one thing from escaping: hope. This meant that however many evils spread over the world, humankind would always have hope.

The Flood

King Deucalion was the son of the Titan Prometheus. He ruled over the men and women of Greece with Queen Pyrrha, the daughter of Pandora and Epimetheus, Prometheus's brother.

The people were happy under Deucalion's rule, but trouble was beginning to brew. Zeus resented the mortals. He had already punished them for obtaining fire against his will. His anger grew as he watched their cities become bigger and busier. "These humans are getting too powerful," he thought, "and they think they are too important."

Zeus sent down torrential rainstorms to rid himself of the humans forever.

The humans prayed and prayed to the gods, but the rain would not end. In desperation, Deucalion asked his father for advice. "Soon, the land will begin to flood," Prometheus told his son. "Build a huge wooden chest and pack it with food—but leave enough space for you and Pyrrha to fit inside. When the water starts to rise, climb inside and stay there until the rain has stopped."

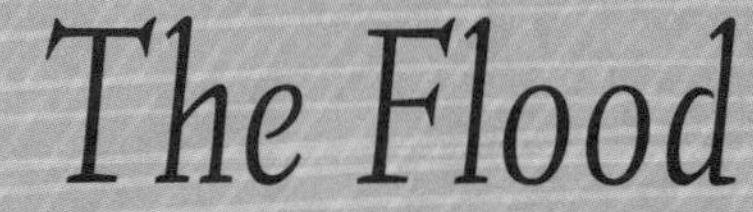

Deucalion and Pyrrha were thrown around on the waves.

Deucalion returned home and hastily set to work on the chest. Soon, rivers began to burst their banks, lakes overflowed, and the seas started to rise. Just as Prometheus had predicted, the flood had come.

The king and queen clambered into the finished chest and floated on the waves as their kingdom disappeared beneath the water. When the people tried to run to the mountains, Zeus threw thunderbolts to break apart the land in front of them.

For nine days, the rain poured down, and Deucalion and Pyrrha were tossed around on the waves.

Finally, the rain stopped and the chest came to rest gently on a small patch of dry land. Zeus watched as Deucalion and Pyrrha climbed out and was impressed by their escape. "I will grant you one wish," he said.

Deucalion asked at once for a new people to rule over. Zeus agreed and threw a stone at Deucalion's feet. From this stone, a new group of humans sprang up. These people lived in peace with the gods.

The stone transformed into a new group of men and women.

Dionysus and the Pirates

Dionysus was the son of Zeus, but his mother was a mortal woman named Semele. Despite being the child of a god, people often mistook Dionysus for a human.

It was on one of these occasions that Dionysus came up against a band of pirates. He wished to travel from the island of Icaria to the island of Naxos, which meant that he needed a ship to take him across the dangerous sea. He went to the harbor and found a captain who was willing to transport him for money—but it was a trap! The captain was the leader of a gang of villainous pirates.

The ship set sail, and soon Naxos was in sight. By now, though, the pirates had decided that they could make more money by selling Dionysus into slavery. They continued sailing, right past the island.

The pirates didn't know whom they were double-crossing.

When Dionysus realized what was happening, he decided to use his powers to play tricks on the troublesome pirates.

First, he made the wooden ship sprout vines of ivy, which wound their tendrils around the boat. Next, he filled the air with mysterious music. “What’s going on?” yelled the pirates, trying to cover their ears. Dionysus then turned the mast and oars of the ship into snakes, which writhed on the deck. Finally, he transformed himself into a menacing lion, which sent the pirates running in fear. One by one, they flung themselves over the side of the boat into the sea below. The moment they hit the water, each pirate transformed into a sleek, gray dolphin.

The pirates turned into dolphins when they hit the waves.

Dionysus found all of this hilariously funny. As he sailed back to Naxos alone, he knew that no one would mistake him for a mortal again.

Orpheus and Eurydice

Orpheus was the most skilled musician on Earth. He sang sweeter than a nightingale, and he could play any instrument expertly.

Apollo gave Orpheus his own lyre to play.

The god Apollo even gave his lyre to Orpheus so that he could hear what music Orpheus would create with it. Orpheus was also married to a young woman named Eurydice, whom he loved with all his heart.

One day, Eurydice was out picking flowers. All was well until she reached for a delicate bloom and startled a poisonous snake, which bit her. When she did not return home, Orpheus went to look for her, but it was already too late.

Eurydice's soul had passed into the underworld.

Orpheus was distraught. From that day on, he played only mournful music. It was filled with so much sadness that even the gods felt pity for him. In fact, they felt so sorry for Orpheus that they allowed him an audience with Hades in the underworld.

"Please, Hades," Orpheus begged, "return Eurydice to me. I can't live without her."

Hades grumbled, "I can't just let every soul out of the underworld because their family asks me to. Imagine the chaos above if I did!"

Luckily, Hades' wife, Persephone, was touched by Orpheus's love for Eurydice. "Can't you see how much he loves her?" she said. "And haven't you heard his music? It's heartbreaking."

Hades was persuaded by his wife. "Leave the underworld," he told Orpheus, "and I will allow Eurydice to follow you. There is just one rule, however: you must not turn around to look at her until you have reached the world above."

Orpheus set off back toward the land of the living, and Eurydice followed him.

At first, Orpheus was overjoyed, but the longer he walked, the more he started to doubt Hades. "What if this is a trick?" he thought. "Or what if Eurydice has lost her way?" As he neared the gates that led out of the underworld, Orpheus could not stop himself from sneaking a glance over his shoulder. There was Eurydice in all her beauty! In a second, however, she had vanished.

Orpheus had failed to follow Hades' instructions, and Eurydice was gone forever. Orpheus was dismayed. His only comfort was that when his own time came to enter the underworld, he would be united with his wife again.

When Orpheus turned to look at Eurydice, she disappeared.

GODDESS

HESTIA

GODDESS OF THE HEARTH

Hestia was responsible for the hearth—the place where a fire is lit in the home. It was her job to keep a fire alight on Mount Olympus at all times. Both Poseidon and Apollo wanted to marry her, but she turned them down, and she chose not to have children.

PARENTS: Cronos and Rhea

CHILDREN: None

SACRED SYMBOLS

VEIL
Hestia was usually seen wearing a veil over her hair.

FIRE
Fire and the lit fireplace represented Hestia's blessing over the household.

BREAD
Bread was baked in the hearth, and so was associated with Hestia.

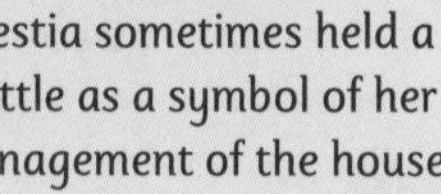

KETTLE
Hestia sometimes held a kettle as a symbol of her management of the house.

HEARTH AND HOME

Hestia was incredibly important to the people of Greece. She was always given the first sacrifice made in the home, regardless of which other gods were being honored. Because the Greeks saw cities as extensions of the home, she also took care of them.

GOD

HERMES

MESSENGER OF THE GODS

Hermes' job on Olympus was to carry the messages of the gods to the mortals on Earth. His sandals and hat had wings, so that he could fly to places quickly. Hermes was also responsible for making sure souls traveled safely to the underworld after people died.

PARENTS: Zeus and Maia

CHILDREN: Many

SACRED SYMBOLS

CROCUS
When his companion Crocus was killed, Hermes turned him into a crocus flower.

TORTOISE
Hermes made the first-ever lyre, a stringed instrument, from the shell of a tortoise.

CADUCEUS
Hermes always carried this staff, which had a pair of snakes twined around it.

TALARIA
These were winged sandals that helped Hermes fly through the air.

DREAM DELIVERER

If the ancient Greeks wished to speak to the gods, they would pray to Hermes before they went to sleep so that he would bring them messages in their dreams. As the god of journeys, he was also worshiped by merchants and travelers.

Midas's Golden Touch

King Midas was the ruler of Phrygia. He was walking in his garden one afternoon when he came across a cold and hungry satyr.

This type of creature had the body of a man and the legs of a goat. The satyr weakly introduced himself as Silenus, and Midas took him inside and gave him food and drink. In return for the kindly king's hospitality, Silenus began to share exciting stories of Dionysus, the god he worshiped.

Dionysus, meanwhile, had been searching for the lost Silenus.

Dionysus was relieved when he found his missing friend, well fed and happy, in Midas's home. "Thank you, Midas," Dionysus said. "Please, make a wish and I will grant it."

Midas began to dream of glorious riches. "I want whatever I touch to turn to gold," he said. Dionysus knew that it was a foolish wish, but he granted it anyway.

Midas couldn't wait to try out his new talent. He reached out to stroke his hand across a tree and

Plates, bowls, and food were turned to gold.

smiled widely as it turned to shining gold.

Midas wandered around his palace, touching the pillars and watching the stone transform beneath his fingers. His servants clapped their hands in delight as he turned one thing after another into the precious yellow metal. Midas ordered a great feast in celebration.

Platters of fruit and jugs of wine were brought by the cartload to the now-golden table.

As soon as Midas tried to eat some of the delicious food, however, he realized his terrible mistake. When he raised the first slice of bread to his mouth, it grew heavy and turned to gold. The same thing happened to the wine in his goblet as it reached his lips. Midas was distraught. "Dionysus, please take back your gift," he cried.

The god appeared and took pity on the king. "Climb the Lydian Hills and wash your hands in the river there," Dionysus told him. "Then you will be free." Midas set off immediately.

At the Lydian River, Midas plunged his hands into the water and the power was washed away. For many years that followed, the gold from Midas's hands could be found on the riverbed.

Eros and Psyche

Psyche was a mortal, famous for her beauty. Admirers came from far and wide to bring her gifts, claiming that she was as pretty as a goddess.

This infuriated Aphrodite, the goddess of beauty, and she decided to punish Psyche out of envy.

Aphrodite went to Eros and instructed him to strike Psyche with an arrow. Eros was the god of love, and his arrows made anyone fall instantly in love with the first thing they saw. "I want you to make sure that Psyche falls in love with a terrifying monster!" Aphrodite added, laughing.

Eros went to find Psyche, but when he caught sight of her he was so struck by her beauty that he dropped his bow.

Eros accidentally scratched his hand with an arrow and fell in love with Psyche himself.

Meanwhile, Psyche's parents went to consult a prophetess about whom their daughter should marry. To their surprise, the prophetess told them, "Psyche is not destined to marry a mortal man. You must leave her on the

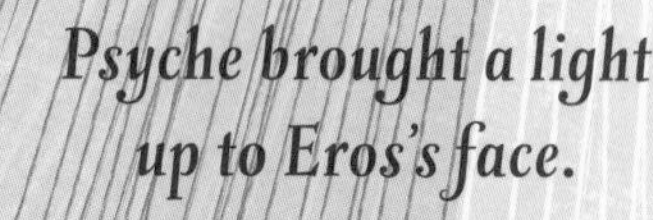

Psyche brought a light up to Eros's face.

side of a mountain and the west wind will carry her away to her husband."

Psyche's parents did just this, and they were amazed when Psyche was lifted up and whisked away on the wind.

The wind carried Psyche to a beautiful meadow, where the smell of the flowers immediately put her to sleep.

During the night, Psyche woke to the sound of a man's voice. "Hello, I am your new husband."

It was Eros, but in the darkness Psyche could not see him. Every night, he visited Psyche and they slept beside one another, but the mysterious man would always be gone before dawn.

Psyche was curious about her husband. One night, she waited for Eros to fall asleep and then lit an oil lamp she had hidden away. When she saw him, she instantly fell in love. As she gazed down, however, a drop of lamp oil spilled onto Eros's torso.

Eros awoke at the pain of the hot oil and fled. When he did not return the next night, Psyche was devastated. She set out in search of him.

Aphrodite saw Psyche looking for Eros and was horrified. She decided to set Psyche three tasks, hoping to keep the pair apart.

That evening, Aphrodite appeared to Psyche. "If you ever want to see your husband again, you must sort these seeds into different piles by morning," she said, pointing to a mound of thousands of grains all mixed together. Then she vanished. The task was impossible for a human alone. Psyche wept. Saddened by Psyche's situation, an ant offered to help her. The ant gathered all the other insects, and among them they were able to separate the seeds before Aphrodite returned.

Aphrodite was amazed that Psyche had completed the task.

"Hmph. Well, now you must fetch me a cutting of wool from the sheep belonging to the sun god, Helios," Aphrodite demanded. These sheep were vicious beasts that could only be tamed by a god, but Psyche set out to the island where they lived. While she was at sea, she heard singing coming from the reeds along the shore. "*Look for wool that has snagged on thorny plants,*" they sang. In this way, Psyche managed to gather enough golden wool without having to confront the sheep.

Even more astounded, Aphrodite went to Psyche a final time and said, "Your last task is to bring me a drop of beauty from Persephone, queen of the underworld."

Psyche traveled to the depths of the underworld and asked Persephone for the gift. Persephone looked at Psyche coldly, then handed her a small box, saying, "This box contains what you need." Overjoyed, Psyche set out for the world above, excited to see her husband again, but her curiosity overwhelmed her and she opened the box.

Inside the box was actually everlasting sleep, and Psyche fell into a deep slumber.

The whole time that Eros had been missing he had, in fact, been imprisoned by Aphrodite. However, he now managed to escape and set out in search of Psyche. He found her asleep on the ground and used his divine powers to wake her. Psyche was delighted to open her eyes and see her husband again.

Eros knew Aphrodite would still be angry, so he requested the help of Zeus, who gave Psyche a small piece of ambrosia. This was the food of the gods and any mortal who ate it became a god themself. Now Aphrodite couldn't keep them apart, and Eros and Psyche were together forever.

Eros and Psyche were together at last.

Arachne

Arachne was an ordinary girl who lived in a mountain town. Her father made his money by dyeing fabric bright and dazzling colors.

Arachne's father had raised her to be a skilled craftswoman, and her talent for weaving became famous. She wove such beautiful tapestries that even nymphs crept out of the forests and rivers to watch her work.

Everyone who saw her tapestries said she must have been blessed by Athena, goddess of weaving.

However, Arachne always insisted that her craft was self-taught and that the goddess had nothing to do with it. "Athena could never weave as striking a tapestry as I can. In fact, I'd like to see her try!" she boasted one day.

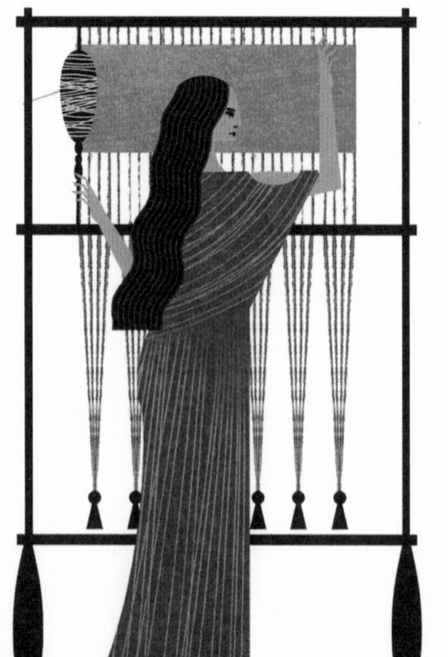

Arachne and Athena were both expert weavers.

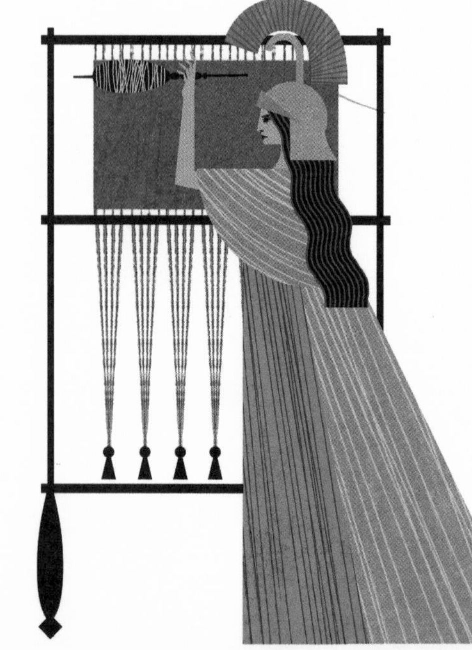

The gods were always listening, and Athena heard Arachne's words. The goddess appeared in an instant. "You have challenged me, mortal," Athena said, "and I accept that challenge." She went straight to the loom next to Arachne, and they both immediately went to work.

The rival weavers soon completed their projects and laid them out for one another to see.

Athena had woven scenes of mortals who gloated to the gods and the punishments they received for doing so. Her golden thread shone as it showed Antigone, who was changed into a stork when she said she had more beautiful hair than Hera's, and many more mortals like her.

Arachne's tapestry, meanwhile, included acts of cruelty committed by the gods on mortals, such as Zeus transforming into a bull and stealing Europa away from her home. Arachne wanted to show that the gods weren't perfect.

Unfortunately, Arachne had forgotten that she could never outdo a goddess.

Furious, Athena tore Arachne's work to shreds, then cast a spell upon the girl. First, all of Arachne's long hair fell out, and then her body shrank. New legs sprang from her sides until she had eight instead of two. Athena had transformed Arachne into a spider, cursed to weave webs forever.

ARES

GOD OF WAR

Ares was the god of war and was always dressed in armor. He never married, but he loved Aphrodite. Ares fathered the Amazons, a race of fearsome female warriors who lived apart from the rest of society.

PARENTS: Zeus and Hera

CHILDREN: The Amazons, Diomedes, the Ismenian dragon, and many more

SACRED SYMBOLS

POISONOUS DRAGON
Ares was father to the Ismenian dragon, which was killed by the hero Cadmus.

DOG
Ares was often accompanied by his hunting dogs.

HELMET
Ares always wore a helmet, ready for battle. It symbolized his role as the god of war.

VULTURE
Vultures eat dead bodies, and they were associated with battlefields.

UNPOPULAR GOD

Ares was particularly associated with the most violent, wild aspects of war. Perhaps because of this, he was one of the least popular gods, and the ancient Greeks dedicated very few temples to him.

GODDESS

ATHENA

GODDESS OF WAR AND WISDOM

Athena was born from Zeus's head, in full armor. As the goddess of war and wisdom, she was responsible for the planning of battles. Her father, Zeus, tried to give her hand to Hephaestus, but she refused to marry anyone.

PARENTS: Zeus and Metis

CHILDREN: None

SACRED SYMBOLS

OWL
Athena was often seen with an owl, which represented wisdom.

OLIVE TREE
Athena introduced the olive tree to Greece. Olives were eaten and used to make oil.

DISTAFF
This is a stick that wool was wound around. It symbolized Athena's reputation as the best weaver.

SPEAR
Athena was always shown carrying a spear, which represented her skill in battle.

ATHENA OF ATHENS

Athena was the main goddess of Athens. The Greeks believed she fought Poseidon for control of the city and was chosen by its citizens when she gave them an olive tree. Olives were an important trade crop for the Athenians.

The Trojan War

Eris was the least popular of the gods. She was the goddess of arguments, and chaos followed her wherever she went.

For that reason, Eris was the only god not to receive an invitation to the wedding of the mortal King Peleus and the sea nymph Thetis. When Eris learned that she had been left out, she was furious. She decided to crash the wedding and cause mischief.

Eris took a single golden apple with her. On her arrival, she threw it at the feet of three goddesses—Hera, Athena, and Aphrodite. "This apple is for the most beautiful," she said. She had made sure to throw it in such a way that it was equally close to each goddess. This started a squabble among the three. They could not agree on who should take the apple.

Each goddess thought of herself as the most beautiful.

Usually, Zeus settled fights among the other gods—but this time he did not want to upset any of the goddesses. He decided that a mortal man would be the judge—Paris, Prince of Troy. Zeus took all three goddesses to Paris and handed him the apple. "Paris, give this apple to the goddess you think is the most beautiful," he demanded.

Hera, Athena, and Aphrodite each tried to convince Paris to pick them.

Paris and Helen ran away in the night.

All three goddesses pleaded with Paris to choose them and promised him great rewards. "I can make you king of the entire world," Hera said; "I can make you the most powerful warrior in all the land," promised Athena; "I will let you marry the most beautiful woman on Earth," Aphrodite announced.

Paris was a romantic at heart, and he could not say no to Aphrodite's offer, so he handed the shining fruit to her. Aphrodite had won the contest, while Paris had won the hand of Helen, queen of Sparta.

Helen was the most beautiful woman in the world.

Helen was, unfortunately, already married. The gods cared very little for the lives of mortals, and Aphrodite had ignored this fact when she promised Helen to Paris. The goddess went with the prince to the city of Sparta where Helen lived. Paris waited until Helen's husband, Menelaus, was away, then went to find her. Helen was surprised by the arrival of the Trojan prince, but Aphrodite made sure she instantly fell in love with him. In the middle of the night, they sneaked away together.

When Menelaus returned to Sparta and discovered that Paris had stolen his wife, he was very angry. He immediately started to gather the largest army Greece had ever seen. He was joined by many heroes, including his brother Agamemnon, king of Mycenae, the crafty Odysseus of Ithaca, and the most fearsome warrior of them all, Achilles.

Achilles was half-mortal, half-god, which made him practically unbeatable in battle.

In the meantime, Paris had taken Helen home to Troy. Paris's family was far from happy. "Please return Helen to Sparta," begged Hector, his heroic elder brother.

"If you don't, you will start a war between us and the Greeks," said Priam, Paris's father. Paris stubbornly refused.

Menelaus was now ready to set off from Greece to claim Helen back. Between them, the soldiers filled more than a thousand ships. The army sailed across the perilous Aegean Sea directly to Troy. However, the city was surrounded by towering stone walls that were impossible to break down, and the Trojans had barred all the gates. The Greeks would have to lay siege to Troy and stop supplies from reaching the city to make the Trojans surrender. The Trojan War had begun.

Menelaus launched a fleet of more than a thousand ships to bring Helen back.

The war dragged on for nine years, but the Trojans wouldn't give in, and, try as they might, the Greeks couldn't break through the city's defenses. The army's frustrated commanders began to fight among themselves. In particular, Achilles and Agamemnon were constantly arguing. Both were convinced they were the other's superior. Their constant squabbles eventually came to a head when Agamemnon stole one of Achilles' favorite slaves, the beautiful Briseis. Achilles was furious. "I refuse to fight alongside that arrogant Agamemnon until he returns Briseis to me."

Achilles waited in his tent for Briseis to be returned. Agamemnon stoutly refused.

The fighting continued, but without Achilles, the Greeks were weak. It began to look like they would be defeated and have to return home. Although his fellow soldiers pleaded with him to return to the battle, Achilles would not budge. Even the man he loved the most, Patroclus, could not convince him.

Patroclus decided to take matters into his own hands. When all the warriors had gone to sleep, he sneaked into Achilles' tent and stole his armor. The next day, he put it on himself and marched into battle disguised as Achilles! The Greeks cheered, and the Trojans trembled in fear.

Prince Hector knew he was the only man who might be able to defeat Achilles, so he charged against him. Patroclus, however, was not as skilled a warrior as Achilles, and Hector killed him with one quick swipe of his sword. As the man fell to the ground, Hector realized it was not Achilles after all.

When Achilles received word that Patroclus had been lost, he was overcome with grief. His misery quickly turned to anger, and he was determined to avenge Patroclus's death. For this reason, and this reason only, he rejoined the war. Achilles and Hector met on the battlefield. Although they were well matched, Achilles was determined to win for Patroclus. Their swords swung and clashed for hours, but, eventually, Achilles managed to plunge his spear into Hector's side. He had slain Troy's greatest warrior.

Hector's death was a great blow to the Trojan army.

Hector's brother Paris was dismayed to hear of Hector's death and wanted revenge himself. Paris wasn't as strong as Achilles, but Achilles did have a weakness. When he was a baby, Achilles' mother had dipped him in the Styx River in the underworld, in the hope of making him invincible. She had held him by his ankle, however, and this part of him didn't touch the magical waters. Therefore, when Paris fired an arrow and hit Achilles' heel, the Greek hero died immediately.

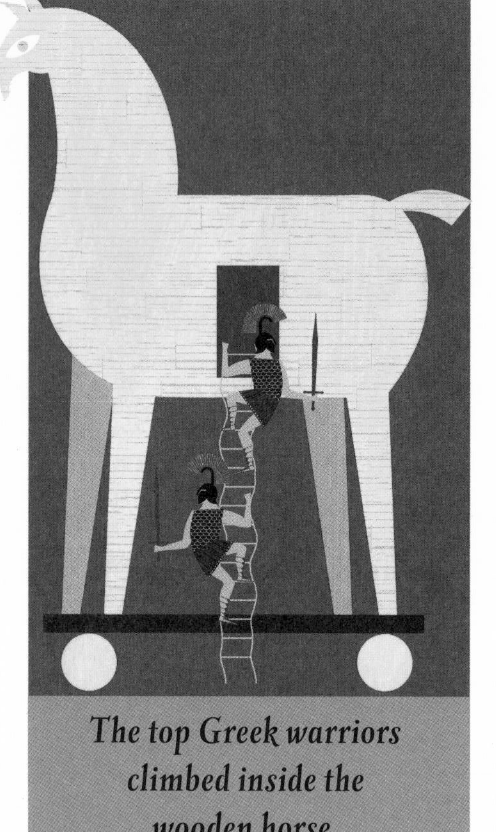

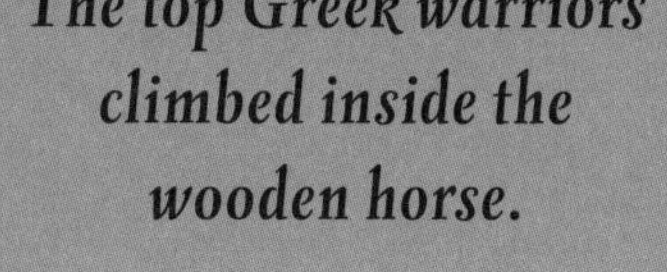

The top Greek warriors climbed inside the wooden horse.

The two armies fought on. During one battle, Paris was slain by a Greek archer. Still, the Trojans did not let Helen return to the Greeks, and the two sides were still evenly matched. It was the clever Greek hero Odysseus who realized the key to victory was to outwit the enemy. Odysseus went to the Greek architect Epeios and said, "Please build me a giant wooden horse. It should be big enough to hold fifty men in full armor in its belly."

Epeios did as he was asked, and the strongest Greek warriors, including Odysseus, hid inside the horse. Meanwhile, the rest of the soldiers abandoned their camp and took to their ships. They did not sail far, however. Odysseus had instructed them, "Go just far enough so you are out of sight of Troy. The Trojans will think we've given up and gone home."

The next day, the Trojans saw the ships had gone and thought the Greeks had left.

Just as Odysseus had planned, the Trojans were ecstatic when they saw the Greek camp deserted. They believed the wooden horse was a gift to the gods from the Greeks, and they decided to bring it inside the city walls. Although some of the Trojans thought they should build a bonfire and burn the horse, others wished to keep it to give to the gods themselves. It was the second group who won.

That day, the streets of Troy were filled with people singing and dancing. Meanwhile, the Greek soldiers lay in wait. When night fell and the last

partygoer had fallen asleep, the band of Greeks climbed out of the horse. “Quick, open the city gates,” commanded Odysseus.

The rest of the Greek army had sailed back to Troy and was waiting outside. The soldiers could now charge into the city, and they had the advantage of surprise.

While the Greeks slaughtered the sleeping Trojan warriors, Menelaus searched for his wife. He found Helen in the Trojan palace, guarded by Paris’s younger brother, Deiphobus. Menelaus killed the Trojan prince and led Helen back to his ship. After 10 years, the war was finally over.

The hidden warriors went to open the gates of Troy and let in the Greek army.

HEROES

Over time, the names of some humans became almost as well known as those of the gods themselves. They were the mythical heroes who had achieved incredible feats through extraordinary skill, bravery, strength, and cunning.

These are the stories of men and women journeying to astonishing places, defeating evil monsters, and saving innocent lives.

Cadmus Builds Thebes

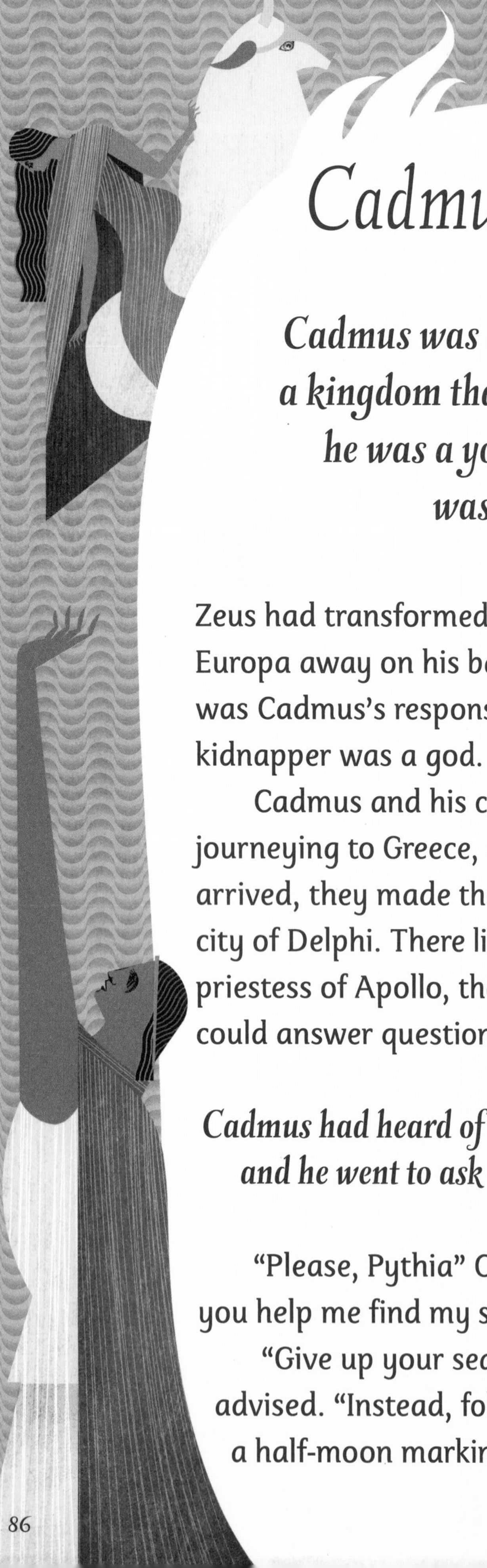

Cadmus was a mortal man from Phoenicia, a kingdom that lay far east of Greece. When he was a young man, his sister Europa was kidnapped by Zeus.

Zeus had transformed himself into a mighty bull and carried Europa away on his back across the sea. As her brother, it was Cadmus's responsibility to rescue Europa, even if her kidnapper was a god.

Cadmus and his crew spent many weeks journeying to Greece, and when they arrived, they made their way to the city of Delphi. There lived the famous priestess of Apollo, the Pythia, who could answer questions about the future.

Cadmus had heard of the Pythia's powers, and he went to ask her for guidance.

"Please, Pythia" Cadmus said, "will you help me find my sister?"

"Give up your search for her," the Pythia advised. "Instead, follow the cow that has a half-moon marking on its body."

Surprised, but trusting the Pythia, Cadmus and his men set off into the fields around Delphi. Sure enough, they soon spotted a cow with a half-moon mark and followed it across the hills. Finally, it slumped down, exhausted.

Cadmus decided to sacrifice the cow to the goddess Athena. He sent some men to fetch water for the ceremony, but when they arrived at the local well they found it guarded by a fearsome dragon.

Cadmus took it upon himself to slay the beast.

Cadmus and the dragon fought sword against claw, but eventually Cadmus saw his opportunity and sliced off the monster's head. Triumphant, he collected the water and returned to his men. What he did not realize was that this was the Ismenian dragon, a child of Ares, the god of war.

Ares was angry and upset. Desperate for the god's forgiveness, Cadmus offered to serve Ares for as long as he needed. For eight long years, Cadmus obeyed Ares' every command, until finally the god released him.

Athena, however, had not forgotten Cadmus's sacrifice. She decided to help him build a city where the cow had died. Cadmus never found his sister Europa, but he did establish the great city of Thebes.

Cadmus built the mighty city of Thebes.

Perseus and Medusa

Danaë was a princess. Her father, Acrisios, was king of Argos, and his worst fear was that she would have a son, because a prophetess had told him that any boy Danaë had would kill him.

To avoid this fate, he locked Danaë in a deep, dank chamber where no one could reach her. No one, that is, except a god. Zeus had fallen in love with Danaë and he sneaked into her prison disguised as a shower of golden rain. Danaë was soon pregnant with his child.

One day, Acrisios heard a loud wailing.

He found that Danaë had given birth to a baby boy, whom she had named Perseus. Acrisios was horrified. He locked his daughter and her child in a heavy wooden chest and threw the chest into the sea, hoping they would drown.

Unfortunately for Acrisios, the chest floated. It bobbed over the sea and came to rest on the island of Seriphos. There, a man named Dictys found it. He unbolted the lid and, to his surprise, found Danaë and Perseus inside. Dictys thought Danaë was very beautiful, and he offered to marry her and raise her son as his own.

One day, years later, Dictys brought Danaë to meet his brother Polydectes, the king of Seriphos.

Dictys was amazed to find Danaë and baby Perseus in the chest.

When he saw her, Polydectes also fell in love with Danaë. He wanted to steal her away from Dictys, but Perseus was a strong young man now, and Polydectes knew he would stand in his way. Polydectes decided to send Perseus on a dangerous mission in the hope that he would not come back. "Perseus, as king of Seriphos, I command you to bring me the head of Medusa," he ordered.

Medusa had once been a mortal, but Athena had cursed her to become a hideous Gorgon—a monster with hair made of slithering snakes. Anyone who looked into her eyes was instantly turned to stone.

Perseus would have to use all of his skill and cunning to defeat Medusa.

First, Perseus traveled to the island where Medusa lived and waited until the dead of night. Then, he carefully walked backward up to her sleeping body, using his polished shield as a mirror so that he didn't have to look directly at her. Finally, he drew his sword and swung it with all his strength to chop off her head.

Perseus grabbed the severed head, writhing with snakes, and stuffed it into a sack. Even now, he was careful not to look at it, as its power remained.

Andromeda was chained to the cliffs.

His task completed, Perseus began his journey back to Seriphos. On the way, he sailed by the kingdom of Aethiopia, ruled by King Cepheus and Queen Cassiopeia. As his ship passed, he saw a woman chained to the rocks. He didn't know it yet, but it was Princess Andromeda.

Cassiopeia had been so proud of her daughter's beauty that she declared: "My daughter is more dazzling than all of the nymphs in the sea." The sea nymphs and their father, Poseidon, took great offense at this. They unleashed a flood upon the kingdom, followed by the sea monster Ketos.

Ketos was a giant serpent with razor-sharp teeth and a taste for human flesh.

Desperate to calm the gods, Cepheus had asked a priestess for help. The priestess told him: "You must sacrifice your daughter to Ketos." So Cepheus had chained Andromeda to the cliffs and left her to die.

As soon as Perseus saw Andromeda, he fell deeply in love, but at that moment, Ketos rose up from the waves and made straight for the princess. Perseus ran at the monster. He dodged and weaved as the slithering beast snapped at him, and he plunged his blade into the monster's heart. With Ketos dead, Perseus rushed to free Andromeda.

Cepheus was eternally grateful to Perseus. He gave his blessing for Andromeda and Perseus to be married, and together they left for Seriphos.

Upon their arrival, however, they found Danaë and Dictys hiding in a temple. Polydectes had gathered a group of men and was attempting to capture Danaë.

Perseus was filled with rage.

He confronted the mob and took Medusa's head from his sack. Holding it by the still-wriggling snakes, he turned its glare on Polydectes. As soon as Polydectes saw the gruesome face, he turned to stone. Now that Polydectes was dead, Dictys and Danaë became king and queen.

Perseus's fame spread, and Acrisios learned that his grandson had survived. In fear, Acrisios moved far away to Thessaly. However, Perseus was set to compete in the athletic games there. When Perseus threw the discus in one event, it veered into the crowd and struck Acrisios from behind, causing him to fall down dead. Prophecies always found a way of coming true.

Polydectes turned to stone when he saw Medusa's head.

The Amazons

The Amazons were a group of warrior women who lived alone, far from any city. They were the daughters of the war god, Ares.

The Amazons dedicated their lives to the art of warfare and were stronger and more fearsome than the most well-trained fighters in Greece. The only times the Amazons had contact with men outside of war were when they journeyed to nearby lands, fell in love, and had children. The women, however, always returned to their home. If an Amazon gave birth to a son, she would leave him to be raised by his father, but any baby girls were welcomed back to live alongside their sisters.

The queen of the Amazons, Myrina, had formed an alliance with another group called the Atlantians.

The Atlantians were under threat from their neighbors, the Gorgons—a group of monstrous winged women with snakes for hair, who often attacked the Atlantians. To protect their friends, the Amazons launched an attack on the Gorgons.

Both sides had large armies. The Amazons, however, had a secret weapon.

The Amazons covered themselves with snakeskin armor made from a breed of giant serpents found only in their homeland. Their scales was stronger than steel. It protected the warriors from their enemies' swords and arrows.

The Amazons fought the Gorgon army for weeks, and both sides lost many of their soldiers. With the advantage of their armor though and under the command of Queen Myrina, the Amazons gained the upper hand. The Gorgons were defeated and the Amazons had saved the Atlantians.

Bellerophon and Pegasus

Bellerophon was a hero on a mission. King Iobates had asked him to slay the monstrous chimaera, which was terrorizing the people of Lycia.

The chimaera had the head and body of a fearsome lion, a scaly tail ending in a dragon's head, and, worst of all, a fire-breathing goat's head on its back.

While on his way to find the chimaera, Bellerophon caught sight of a magnificent winged horse drinking from a stream. This was, in fact, the magical horse Pegasus. He had conjured the stream using the powers given to him by his father, Poseidon. Whenever Pegasus stomped his hooves on the ground, a spring of water would appear.

Seeing Pegasus gave Bellerophon an idea.

Bellerophon sneaked up quietly and managed to mount the horse. Pegasus bucked and reared, but Bellerophon clung on. Finally, Pegasus grew calmer and Bellerophon spurred him forward, into the sky. Together, they flew straight to Lycia.

When they arrived at the chimaera's lair, Bellerophon plotted a clever attack. He flew Pegasus high into the air, so

Pegasus and Bellerophon dived close to the fearsome chimaera.

they could circle the chimaera from above. Then they dived down quickly, weaving and wheeling to avoid the jets of fiery breath from the angry monster.

Between the chimaera's attacks, Pegasus darted in closer so Bellerophon could draw his bow and fire his arrows, while ducking out of the way of the snapping dragon tail. Eventually, one of Bellerophon's arrows struck the chimaera's neck, and it dropped to the floor, dead.

King Iobates was delighted. He gave Bellerophon permission to marry his daughter, Princess Philonoe, and made him heir to the kingdom. There, Bellerophon ruled, with Pegasus as his steed.

APOLLO

GOD OF MUSIC

Apollo was the twin brother of Artemis. When he was born, he was supposedly holding a golden sword in one hand. Apollo was the god of many things, including music, healing, and oracles—places where people heard their future. He could even make mortals see the future.

PARENTS: Zeus and Leto

CHILDREN: Orpheus and many more

SACRED SYMBOLS

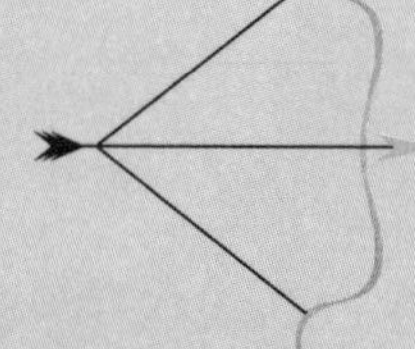

GOLDEN BOW
Apollo carried a golden bow and arrows made for him by Hephaestus.

SWAN
Apollo flew on the back of a swan to get around.

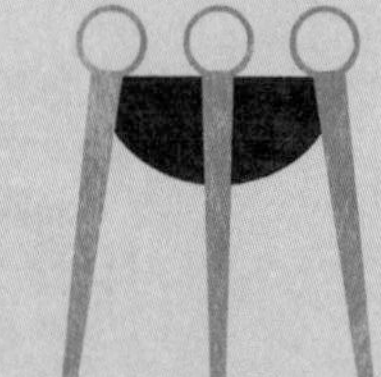

TRIPOD
Apollo's most powerful priestess, the Pythia, sat on a sacred tripod.

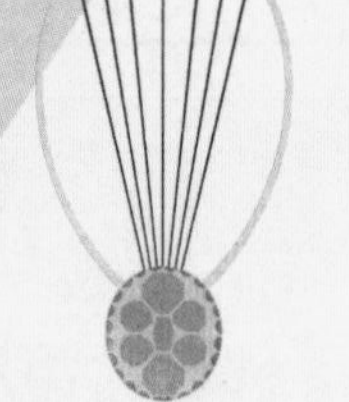

LYRE
Apollo was skilled with many musical instruments, but he favored the stringed lyre.

SEEING THE FUTURE

Apollo's most famous temple was in Delphi, where his greatest priestess, the Pythia, lived. People, including kings and queens, would travel great distances to see the Pythia. She would give them advice and tell their future.

ARTEMIS

GODDESS OF HUNTING

Artemis was the twin sister of Apollo. She was the goddess of hunting and no one could beat her with a bow and arrow. Artemis never married and didn't stay on Mount Olympus, preferring to live in the forest with her specially chosen group of female huntresses.

PARENTS: Zeus and Leto

CHILDREN: None

SACRED SYMBOLS

DEER
Artemis often wore a deerskin as a cloak.

DOG
Artemis kept hunting dogs that helped her catch prey.

BEAR
The young women who served in Artemis's temples were known as "little bears."

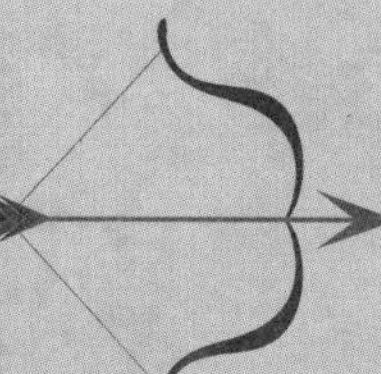

BOW AND ARROW
Artemis always carried her trusty bow. She was a very skilled archer.

GIRLS' GODDESS

Artemis was seen as protector of young girls before they were wed. Some of these women would travel to Artemis's temples and serve the goddess before returning home to get married. There, they would compete in races, dance together, and make sacrifices to Artemis.

Jason and the Argonauts

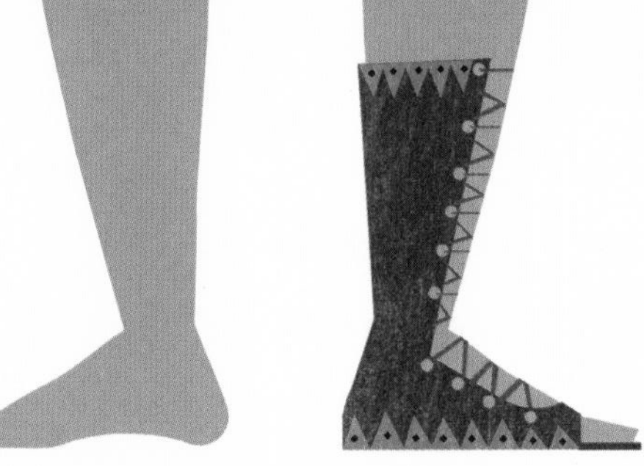

Pelias was the ruler of Iolcus, but he was an anxious king. An oracle had warned him that one of his relatives would one day steal his throne.

The prophetess had told him: “The man who will challenge you will arrive on your doorstep wearing only one sandal.” From that day, Pelias had been on high alert. Then Pelias’s nephew Jason returned after being away for a long time. On his way back to the palace, Jason had fallen crossing a river and lost one of his sandals in the fast-flowing water.

When Pelias saw Jason, he was struck with fear. He made a plan to get rid of Jason.

“Dear nephew,” Pelias told Jason, “there is a sheep’s fleece made of pure gold that belongs to King Aeëtes of Colchis, and I want it. Will you go and fetch it for me?” Jason was an adventurer at heart, and he agreed at once to go. What Jason did not know was how dangerous a journey it would be. Pelias had chosen this mission specifically because he believed there was no chance Jason, or his men, would survive it.

Jason gathered an impressive crew, including the mighty Herakles, son of Zeus, and the famed musician Orpheus. Together, they set sail on a sturdy ship called the Argo and headed for Colchis.

On their voyage, they stopped in the kingdom of Thrace. This was the home of the prophet Phineus. He had once been a great ruler, but he had angered Zeus when he shared too much of the future with his people. As a punishment, Zeus took away his sight and sent terrible monsters called harpies to torment him.

Each harpy had the head of a woman but the body of a bird.

The harpies circled Phineus constantly, and whenever he tried to eat they swooped down and stole the food right out of his hands.

When Jason and his men came across the blind prophet, they took pity on him. Two of the crew waited for Phineus to start his meal and when the harpies flew down to steal it, they ran at them, swords drawn. The monsters were scared off for good. To show his gratitude, Phineus shared with the crew the fastest route to Colchis.

Whenever Phineus tried to eat, the harpies stole the food from his hands.

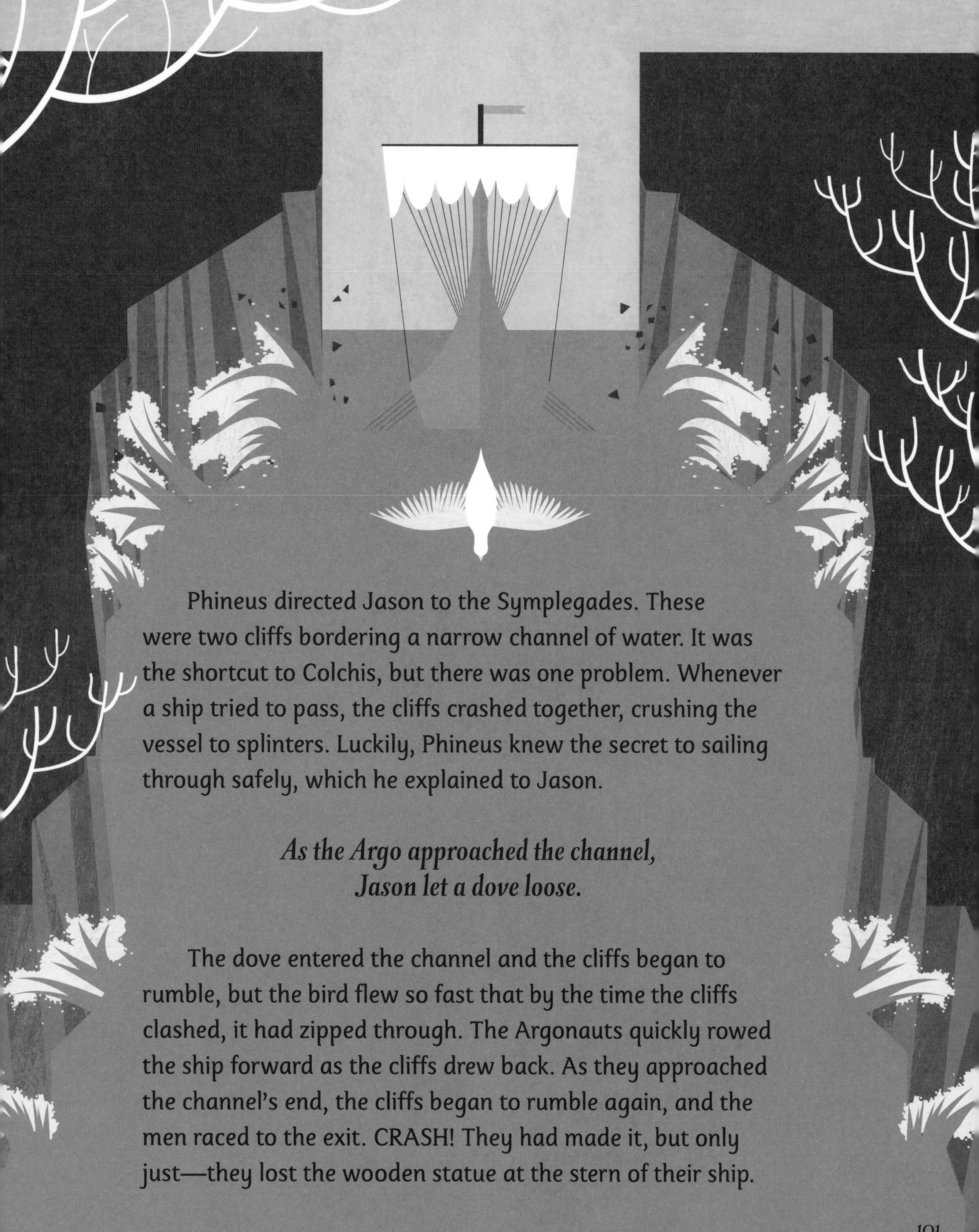

Phineus directed Jason to the Symplegades. These were two cliffs bordering a narrow channel of water. It was the shortcut to Colchis, but there was one problem. Whenever a ship tried to pass, the cliffs crashed together, crushing the vessel to splinters. Luckily, Phineus knew the secret to sailing through safely, which he explained to Jason.

As the Argo approached the channel,
Jason let a dove loose.

The dove entered the channel and the cliffs began to rumble, but the bird flew so fast that by the time the cliffs clashed, it had zipped through. The Argonauts quickly rowed the ship forward as the cliffs drew back. As they approached the channel's end, the cliffs began to rumble again, and the men raced to the exit. CRASH! They had made it, but only just—they lost the wooden statue at the stern of their ship.

Medea gave Jason a potion to help with his task.

When Jason and his crew finally landed on the coast of Colchis, they went straight to the palace. As soon as they arrived, Jason asked for an audience with the king and found himself standing in front of Aeëtes and his family.

The mischievous god of love, Eros, was watching. He decided to play a trick.

Eros made Aeëtes' daughter Medea fall passionately in love with Jason. She hung on Jason's every word when he spoke to her father. "Aeëtes," said Jason, "I have been sent here to ask for the golden fleece. I cannot return home without it. I will do anything you ask of me in exchange for it."

At this, Aeëtes laughed nastily. "Fine," he said snidely. "Tomorrow you will have a chance to win the fleece. I want you to harness the fire-breathing bulls I keep. Then you must plow a field outside my palace and sow this bag of dragon's teeth." Jason accepted Aeëtes' challenge, but Medea was very worried.

Luckily, Medea was no ordinary princess.

She was also a witch and skilled in magic. That night, she went to find Jason. "I wish to help you," she said, "but you must make me a promise first. My father will be furious I aided you, so you must take me home with you and make me your wife."

"Of course!" said Jason, glad of the clever Medea's assistance.

Medea gave Jason a bottle. "Spread this potion on your armor and it will protect you from harm," she explained.

The next day, everyone gathered to watch Jason attempt the impossible task. Protected by Medea's potion, however, Jason was able to approach the fire-breathing bulls without being burned, harness them, and plow the field. Next, he sprinkled the dragon's teeth on the upturned soil. Suddenly, where the teeth had fallen, soldiers sprung from the ground!

Where each tooth was planted, an armed soldier climbed out of the ground.

Jason had to think—and act—quickly. He spotted a rock on the ground and flung it into the middle of the armed men. It hit one of the soldiers on the back. The soldier spun around, glared at his nearest neighbor, and drew his sword. Confused, the men attacked each other, and soon a huge fight broke out. Jason was able to cut down the remaining soldiers easily.

Aeëtes was furious. "You must have cheated!" he said. "If you want the fleece, go and get it. It is guarded by a dragon at the edge of my kingdom. Let's see you get past that."

Medea sprinkled a sleeping potion into the dragon's eyes.

Medea went with Jason to the cliffs where the dragon dwelled. Once again, she brought a potion. She crept up to the dragon and sprayed the liquid into its eyes, sending the monster into a deep sleep.

Jason sneaked behind the snoring dragon and grabbed the golden fleece from the tree on which it hung.

Together, he and Medea ran to the shore where Jason's men were waiting. They boarded the ship and the crew set sail without delay.

After many months at sea, Jason and his new wife arrived back in Iolcus. Jason had been gone so long, however, that everyone had assumed he was dead, and his heartbroken parents had passed away. The elderly King Pelias was happy, though, because he thought he was safe.

When Jason went to give the fleece to Pelias, the king was disappointed to see him, but he accepted it gladly. He didn't even mention Jason's parents. Jason was enraged. He went to Medea and together they hatched a plot for revenge.

Even so far from home, Medea's skills as a witch were well-known, and she used this to her advantage. She went to Pelias's daughters. "I can teach you a spell to make your father young again," she promised.

"How?" the girls asked eagerly.

"It's very simple. You must cut your father into tiny pieces and boil them in water," Medea replied.

The princesses were unsure at first, but Medea demonstrated her spell by cutting up a ram and turning it into a lamb.

The girls boiled up the pieces of King Pelias in a cauldron.

Now, they were convinced.

Pelias's daughters were not witches, however, and when they attempted Medea's spell their father did not come back to life as the lamb had done.

With Pelias dead, his son Acastos succeeded him on the throne. His first decision as king was to banish Jason and Medea from the kingdom, so the couple traveled to Corinth, where they had two sons.

Still, as the years went by, Jason dreamed of returning to Iolcus.

Then Jason learned that one of the other Argonauts, Peleus, was planning to attack Acastos. Jason rushed to join him in the fight. Acastos was easily defeated, and for his help, Jason became ruler of Iolcus. The prophecy that his uncle, Pelias, had feared had finally come true.

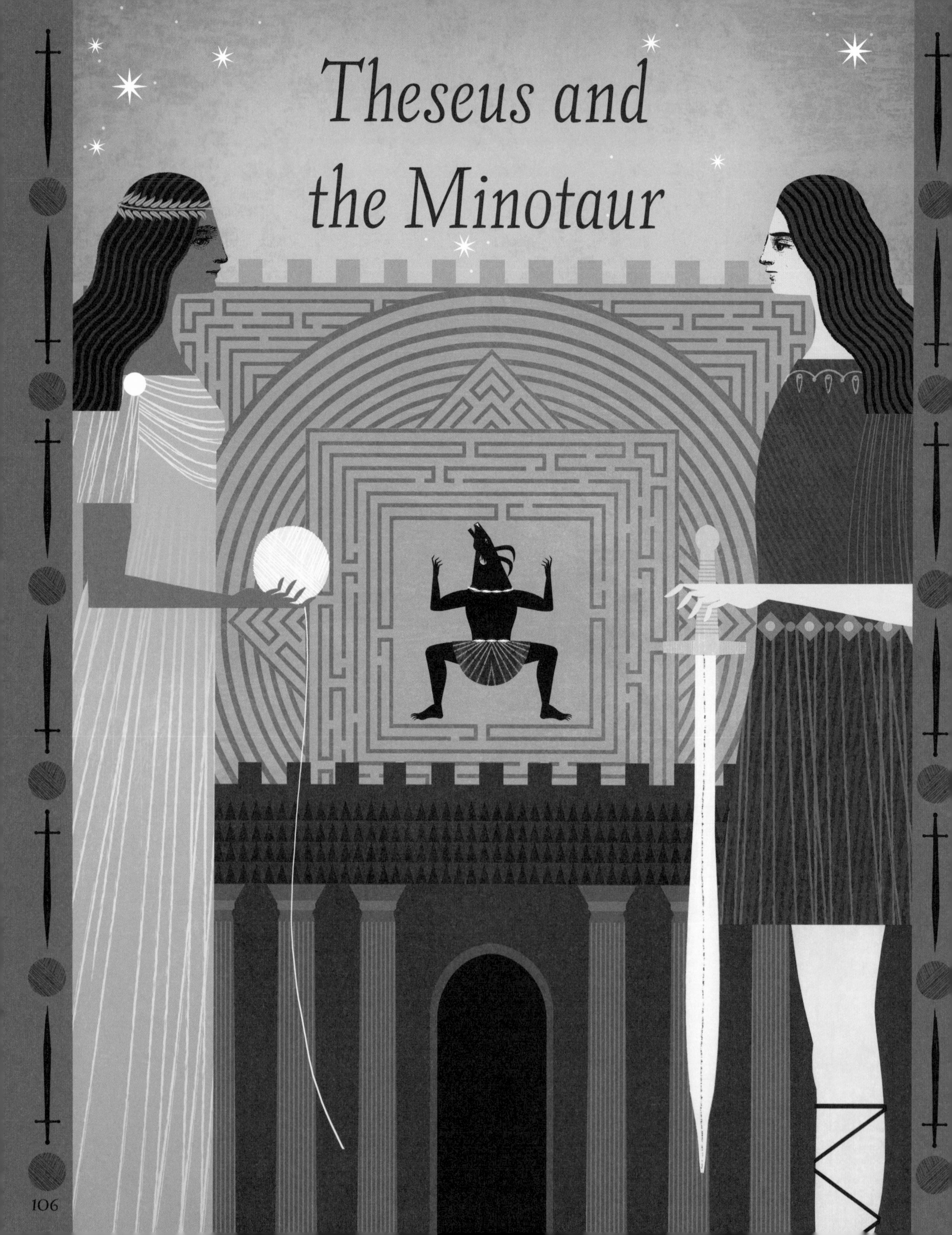

Theseus and the Minotaur

King Minos ruled the island of Crete, but he was a greedy monarch, and he had been trying to conquer the Greek city of Athens for some time.

After many years of fighting, the Athenians ran short of food and they surrendered to Minos. The victorious king demanded that each year the Athenians send to him seven boys and seven girls so that they could be fed to the Minotaur—a dreadful beast, half-man, half-bull, that Minos kept trapped in an endless maze known as the Labyrinth. The Labyrinth prevented the monster from terrorizing the people of Crete, but it also stopped the boys and girls from escaping.

No one had ever made their way out of the Labyrinth alive.

Three years after Athens had surrendered, the Athenian prince Theseus had had enough: "This year I am going to Crete to kill the Minotaur once and for all!" he announced.

His father, King Aegeus, was worried. "Theseus, promise me that if you survive, you will fly white sails on your ship, so I can see you are returning safely," he asked.

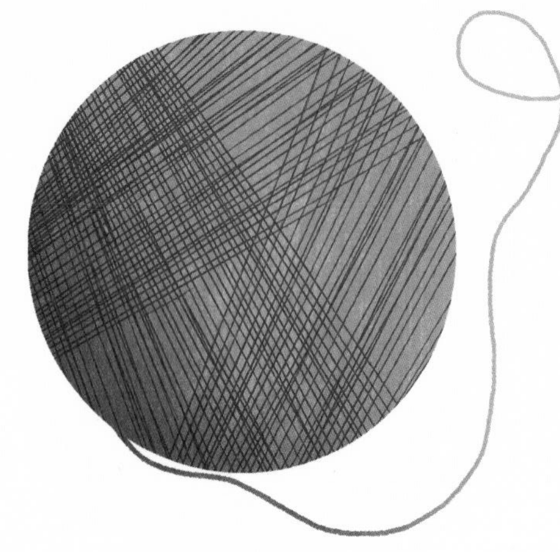

So, Theseus boarded the ship to Crete with the other thirteen boys and girls who were to be sacrificed that year. On his arrival, Minos's daughter Princess Ariadne caught sight of the handsome young prince and immediately fell in love.

In the dead of night, Ariadne crept out of her room to visit Theseus.

"Theseus," she whispered, "if I help you escape the Labyrinth, will you promise to take me back to Athens with you?" Theseus agreed, so Ariadne handed him a ball of string. "Take this string and tie one end of it at the entrance of the Labyrinth. Unwind the rest as you walk through," she explained, "then you can follow it back out to leave."

The monstrous Minotaur was half-bull, half-man.

The next day, Theseus was led to the start of the Labyrinth. He hunted for the Minotaur through the twisting, turning passages, making sure to leave a trail of string behind him. Suddenly, he heard a terrifying snort and the beast charged around a corner. The Minotaur had the body of a huge man and the head of a bull, complete with long, curved horns. Theseus drew his sword. The Minotaur was strong, but it couldn't move as quickly as Theseus in the narrow passage. Theseus darted behind it and swung his sword with all his might. The Minotaur fell to the floor, lifeless.

King Minos was furious, but Theseus took Ariadne away on his ship, planning to make her his queen. During the voyage, however, Ariadne was spotted by the god Dionysus. He fell in love with the princess and took her as his own wife instead.

Theseus had no power over a god.

The prince was devastated to have lost his bride, and in his grief, he forgot his father's instructions. When he sailed into Athens, the sails on his ship were black. Thinking his son had been killed, the king threw himself from the palace walls. Theseus returned having freed his people but lost those he loved the most.

King Aegeus saw the black sails of the ship and thought his son was dead.

Minos was enraged at the loss of both the Minotaur and his daughter. Looking for someone to blame, he remembered the inventor of the Labyrinth, Daedalus. Minos had brought Daedalus to Crete to design the complicated maze, but now it was useless.

As a punishment, the king forbade Daedalus and his son, Icarus, from leaving Crete. However, Daedalus was a clever man who could make use of practically anything around him. With the help of his son, he went in search of as many discarded feathers, of all colors and sizes, as he could find on the island. He then used beeswax to stick the feathers together. Once he had finished, Daedalus held up his handiwork and showed it to Icarus.

Daedalus had made two giant pairs of wings.

"We can use these to fly far away from the island and Minos," Daedalus explained. Icarus was filled with excitement at the idea of flying. "Whatever you do, though," Daedalus warned his son, "don't fly too close to the sun. If you do, the wax that holds the wings together will melt."

Daedalus and Icarus put on their wings and began to run while flapping their arms. Soon, their feet left the ground. As they flew into the sky, they saw Minos gazing up at them in horror and laughed.

The heat of the sun melted the wax in Icarus's wings, and he began to fall.

Their joy was short-lived, however. Daedalus flew calmly, gliding over the sparkling sea, but Icarus was eager to test his wings.

In his excitement, Icarus forgot his father's warning.

Icarus swooped and soared, flying higher and higher. He did not notice that the wax that held his wings together was beginning to melt in the heat of the sun. He began to fall. "Icarus!" Daedalus yelled when he saw what was happening, but it was too late. Icarus splashed into the waves below and died, leaving his father to fly on alone.

APHRODITE

GODDESS OF LOVE AND BEAUTY

Aphrodite was the goddess of love. She was married to Hephaestus, although this was not through her own choice, as she really loved Ares. She helped the heroes who worshiped her, such as Hippomenes and Paris, win the women they loved.

PARENTS: Ouranos

CHILDREN: Many

SACRED SYMBOLS

SCALLOP SHELL
Aphrodite was born fully grown in a scallop shell from the sea.

RED ROSE
When Aphrodite pricked her finger on a white rose, her blood turned the petals red.

DOVE
Aphrodite's worshipers purified her temples by sacrificing doves.

GOLDEN APPLE
The golden apple was a prize awarded to Aphrodite as the most beautiful goddess.

LOVED BY ALL

In Athens, Aphrodite was celebrated at a woman-only festival where her worshipers would dance and sing on the roofs of the city throughout the night. It was believed that Aphrodite might punish those who did not worship her and who avoided love.

GOD

HEPHAESTUS

GOD OF SMITHS AND VOLCANOES

Hephaestus was skilled in metalwork, so all of the other gods came to him for their armor and weaponry. He walked with a limp because his stepfather, Zeus, had thrown him from Mount Olympus as a child.

PARENTS: Hera

CHILDREN: Many

SACRED SYMBOLS

VOLCANO
Hephaestus's workshops were believed to be found inside the bellies of volcanoes.

TONGS
Hephaestus was usually seen holding tongs for grasping hot metal.

HAMMER
Hephaestus often carried a hammer, sometimes striking it against his anvil to make armor or weaponry.

DONKEY
Hephaestus rode a donkey instead of a horse.

VOLCANIC WORKSHOP

As the god of crafts, Hephaestus was most popular with those who worked with their hands. The Greeks believed that volcanoes were Hephaestus's workshops. Any volcanic noises and fumes were thought to come from him forging his creations inside.

The Twelve Labors of Heracles

Heracles was the baby son of Zeus and a mortal woman named Alcmene. Hera, Zeus's wife, was jealous of his love for Heracles, so she decided to get rid of the child.

Hera conjured two huge snakes and sent them to kill Heracles. The serpents slid into the baby's crib but, unaware of the danger he was in, Heracles playfully grabbed them and accidentally squeezed the life out of them. Alcmene woke to find her baby holding two dead snakes and realized that Zeus had passed onto him a godlike strength.

As Heracles grew, so did his superhuman strength.

Heracles's power made him famous, and many people came to him for help. Creon, the king of Thebes, asked Heracles to defend his kingdom against an invading army. When Heracles drove away Creon's enemies single-handedly, the king allowed him to marry his daughter Megara.

Megara and Heracles were happily married and had three children. Hera, however, still hated Heracles and now saw an opportunity to punish him. She sent a curse that drove Heracles mad. In this state, Heracles did not recognize his wife or children and, believing them to be a threat, killed all four.

1

When the curse wore off and Heracles realized what he had done, he was devastated. He decided to go to the Pythia for advice. The Pythia was a priestess of Apollo, famous for her wisdom. “You must go to King Eurystheus,” she told him. “If you complete the tasks he gives you, then you will be forgiven and made immortal like your father, Zeus.”

Heracles went straight to Eurystheus’ palace. However, the king was one of Hera’s most loyal worshipers. Eurystheus agreed to give Heracles 12 tasks to complete, but the king had no intention of making the labors easy.

The first task Eurystheus set was to slay the Nemean lion. He wanted the beast’s skin because no weapon could pierce it. When Heracles tried to shoot the lion with arrows, each one bounced off its golden fur. Instead, Heracles jumped onto the roaring cat’s back and strangled it with his bare hands.

Heracles carried the huge lion back to the palace.

When Eurystheus saw him approaching the gates, he was terrified by Heracles’s might and refused to meet him. Eurystheus sent a messenger to tell Heracles what his next task was, and that he could keep the lion’s skin.

Heracles wrestled the lion to the ground.

2

Heracles's second task was even more difficult than the first. He was sent to kill the Lernaean hydra—a terrifying monster with nine snakelike heads and a scaly body.

The hydra lived in the swamps surrounding Lerna, where it devoured the cattle of the local farmers.

Heracles invited his nephew Iolaos to join him on this task, and together they rode to the hydra's marshy lair. They crept up behind the monster and Heracles swished his sword, chopping off one of the hydra's heads. However, no sooner had the head fallen to the ground, than two more heads grew back in its place. Heracles tried again, but the same thing happened.

Iolaos had an idea. He started a fire while Heracles battled the enraged hydra and heated his sword until it glowed red-hot. Iolaos then followed Heracles, burning the stump of each head as soon as Heracles had lopped it off, which stopped any more from growing back. Together, the two men worked to defeat the hydra and complete the second task.

Annoyed that Heracles had succeeded, Eurystheus made the tasks increasingly difficult...

3 CATCHING THE GOLDEN HIND

The golden hind was a female deer belonging to the goddess Artemis. It had golden horns and was faster than any other creature on Earth. Heracles had to catch it alive but, unable to outrun it, he shot an arrow at the creature to make it stop. Artemis believed Heracles had tried to kill her beloved pet and would not let him touch it.

Only when Heracles promised not to harm the deer again did she allow him to borrow it.

4 CAPTURING THE ERYMANTHIAN BOAR

The Erymanthian boar was a huge, fierce beast with long, sharp tusks. Heracles had to capture it. His friend Chiron, a centaur, advised him to lure the boar onto snowy ground, where it would get stuck. The plan worked and Heracles managed to catch it. When he arrived back at Eurystheus's palace, however, the king was so frightened of the boar he hid in a large vase until Heracles took it away.

5 CLEANING THE AUGEAN STABLES

Heracles's fifth task was to clean the stables of King Augeus, who owned thousands of cows. Their stables were disgustingly filthy. Heracles had an idea, however, and offered to clean the entire stables in a day, in exchange for some of the cattle. Augeus laughed and accepted the suggestion on the spot.

Heracles proceeded to divert the local river, which flowed through the stables, washing away all of the muck in one great rush.

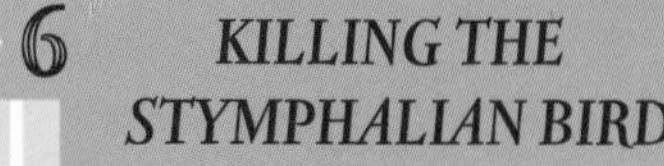

6 KILLING THE STYMPHALIAN BIRDS

Next, Heracles had to rid Lake Stymphalis of an enormous flock of birds that ate humans. He couldn't get near the birds on the lake, so he asked for Athena's help. She gave him a set of loud castanets, which he took to the top of a nearby mountain. When he clapped them, their sound echoed through the valley below. The noise frightened the birds into flight and Heracles was able to shoot them down with arrows.

7 CATCHING THE CRETAN BULL

On the island of Crete, King Minos kept a ferocious fire-breathing bull that he had stolen from Poseidon. On the orders of Eurystheus, Heracles went to steal the beast from Minos himself.

Heracles had to fight the terrifying bull, only narrowly escaping its sharp horns and kicking hooves, but he managed to capture it. He took it to Eurystheus who, once he had laid eyes on the bull, allowed it to be set free.

8 STEALING THE MARES OF DIOMEDES

Heracles' eighth challenge was to take the horses of Diomedes, son of Ares. These were no ordinary horses, though—they ate people alive. With a team of two others, Heracles was able to wrestle the horses from their stables. Diomedes saw that they were gone, however, and chased Heracles. The two men fought and Diomedes was killed. Heracles returned triumphant to Eurystheus's palace.

9 TAKING HIPPOLYTA'S BELT

The Amazons were a group of mighty female warriors. Eurystheus sent Heracles to steal the belt of the Amazon queen, Hippolyta, but she liked Heracles and agreed to give it to him. Hera was furious at this and disguised herself as Hippolyta to trick the rest of the Amazons into attacking Heracles.

Heracles believed that Hippolyta had betrayed him and killed her before fleeing with the belt.

10 STEALING THE CATTLE OF GERYON

The tenth labor was to steal the cattle of Geryon, a giant with the body of three men attached at the waist. When Heracles landed on Geryon's island, he began to herd the cattle away, but he was attacked by the giant's dog, Orthrus. He killed the hound, but the noise alerted Geryon. They fought, and Heracles killed Geryon by shooting one of his heads with an arrow. He then sailed away with the cattle.

... but Heracles completed the next eight labors easily. Eurystheus was more determined than ever to make him fail.

Atlas was doomed to hold up the sky as a punishment for fighting Zeus.

As each of his other plans had failed, crafty Eurystheus decided for the eleventh labor to send Heracles to fetch an apple from the tree of the Hesperides. This was not an easy task. The tree had been a gift to Zeus and Hera on their wedding day, and its fruit shone pure gold. It was guarded by the Hesperides—four fearsome female warriors.

Heracles would have to get past the Hesperides in order to take an apple.

It would be impossible to defeat the Hesperides in a fight, but Heracles had a plan. He went to their father, Atlas, a Titan who was tasked with holding the weight of the sky on his shoulders. "Why not let me hold up the sky to give you a rest," said Heracles, "and in exchange will you ask your daughters to give me a golden apple?" Excited to have a break, Atlas agreed.

When he returned, though, Atlas was reluctant to take the sky back. "I could take the apple to Eurystheus for you?" he asked.

Heracles saw this was a trick. "Okay," he said, "but could you take the sky back for just a moment while I make a cushion for my head?" As soon as Atlas had put the apple on the ground and taken the sky back, Heracles grabbed the fruit and ran.

12

Eurystheus had been thwarted every time. For the final task, he sent Heracles to do the impossible—to go to the underworld itself and steal Hades' dog, Cerberus. This was no ordinary hound. Cerberus had three heads and a scaly dragon's tail.

Rather than anger Hades, Heracles decided to speak to him directly. He went to Hades' palace and asked, "May I borrow your dog, Cerberus, if I swear to return him afterward?" Hades was unsure, but his wife, Persephone, felt sympathy for the hero and persuaded Hades to compromise.

"You may take my dog for a while," Hades told Heracles, "but only if you can catch him without using your weapons."

When Heracles approached Cerberus, all three of the dog's heads snarled.

Heracles wrestled Cerberus with all his might. Even when the dog bit him, he did not let go. Eventually, the dog lost consciousness and Heracles carried him away. Eurystheus was astonished when he saw the monstrous hound, and when Cerberus stirred, the king ran away. Heracles had completed all 12 labors! Just as the Pythia had said, Heracles became immortal and went to join the gods on Mount Olympus.

Odysseus's Voyage

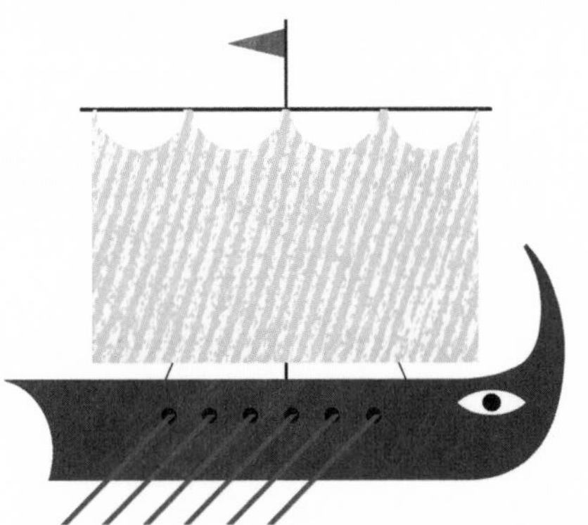

After the Trojan War ended, the Greek heroes who had fought at Troy began their journeys home. Odysseus was the king of an island named Ithaca.

Odysseus was desperate to set sail and return to his wife and son, whom he had not seen in 10 long years. Yet, his voyage home would be far from straightforward.

Odysseus and his crew set out across the sea, but before long they encountered trouble. In search of water, they landed their ships on an island—without knowing it was home to the Cyclops Polyphemus. The Cyclopes were one-eyed giants, a group of whom lived on a collection of small islands. Spotting a large cave up ahead, the crew went to explore and found signs that someone was living there. While they were still inside, they heard a flock of bleating sheep approaching.

Odysseus's men were horrified to see an enormous Cyclops driving his flock toward them.

It was Polyphemus returning with his herd. The Cyclops ushered his sheep into the cavern and pushed a huge boulder into place across the cave entrance, trapping everyone inside. It was only then that he spotted Odysseus and his men staring up at him.

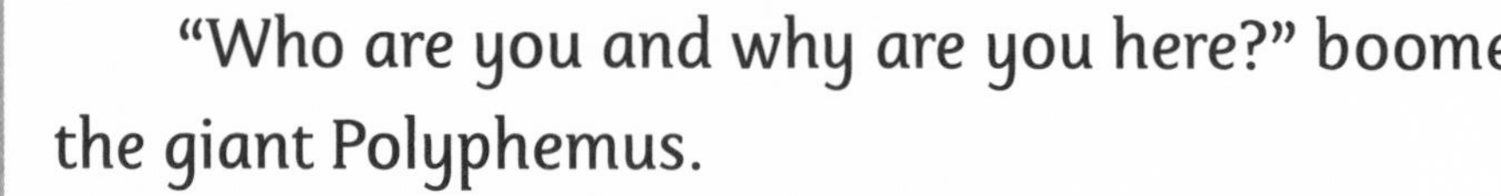

"Who are you and why are you here?" boomed the giant Polyphemus.

Odysseus was a cunning man, and he had his answer ready. "My name is Nobody and these are my men," he said. "We hoped you would share your home with us for the night."

At these words, the Cyclops sneered. He swiped up two of Odysseus's men from the ground and ate them whole. The rest of the men screamed in horror, but Odysseus stayed calm and watched as Polyphemus lay down and went to sleep.

In the morning, the Cyclops left with his sheep, but kept the men trapped in the cave. The next night, the grisly process was repeated, with another two of Odysseus's men becoming the monster's dinner.

This time Odysseus had a plan.

Polyphemus drank the bottle of wine all at once.

"Would you like some wine to wash down your meal?" Odysseus asked, offering the Cyclops a bottle he had brought from the ship. Polyphemus greedily drank the entire bottle in one gulp. What he didn't know was that the wine was very, very strong—it was meant to be mixed with lots of water to dilute it. The effects of the drink were instant. Polyphemus swayed on the spot, then collapsed to the floor.

With the Cyclops impossible to wake, Odysseus ordered the crew to sharpen a long branch he had found in the cave. When it was sharp and spiked, they heaved it onto their shoulders and rammed it into the sleeping giant's eye.

The crew drove the sharpened branch into the Cyclops' eye.

"AHHH!" Polyphemus awoke at the sudden pain. Blinded, he searched for Odysseus's men with his hands, but they were hiding. Polyphemus then began to shout for help from the other Cyclopes who lived nearby. "Nobody has blinded me!" he yelled over and over, using the name Odysseus had given him. The other Cyclopes didn't understand and thought Polyphemus had gone crazy, so they ignored his cries.

When morning came, Polyphemus had to let his sheep out to graze, but he did not want to free the men. He opened the mouth of his cave only a crack, and one by one felt the fluffy backs of his sheep as they left. Crafty Odysseus ordered each of his men to hang onto the belly of a sheep so they would not be felt by the Cyclops, and soon they were free. They ran back to their ship and set sail across the sea.

Odysseus's men clung onto the bellies of the sheep.

After his encounter with Polyphemus, Odysseus was wary. When he and his surviving crew members arrived on the island of Aeaea and spotted a lone house, Odysseus decided to send just a few of his men to investigate.

This was the home of the powerful witch Circe.

When the men reached the house, Circe greeted them warmly. “Come inside, weary travelers, and let me feed you,” she offered. They excitedly agreed.

Circe laid out platters piled high with fine food, and the hungry men stuffed themselves. They were startled, however, when their bodies began to change. Their bellies grew, their hands sprouted hooves, and, finally, their noses turned into flat, wet snouts.

“OINK!”

Odysseus's men grew hooves, snouts, and long ears.

They had turned into enormous pigs! Circe laughed, then drove them into a pen behind her house.

When his men did not return, Odysseus set out in search of them. On his way to Circe's house, the god Hermes appeared before him. Hermes liked Odysseus and wanted to warn him. "Be careful, Odysseus," said Hermes. "This is the home of the witch Circe and she has turned your men into pigs. To rescue them, you need to take this root and mix it into the food Circe offers. It will protect you from the same fate."

Hermes appeared in front of Odysseus.

Thanking the god, Odysseus continued on his way. At Circe's house, he too was invited in to eat, but he mixed the magical root with his meal. Circe was very surprised when he did not change into a pig. Instead, Odysseus challenged her, "Circe, if you do not restore my men to me, I will kill you!"

Circe was afraid. "If he can resist my spells, he must be very powerful," she thought. "Please, forgive me," she begged. "I will turn your men back into humans, and you can rest in my home as long as you like." Odysseus agreed, and they stayed with Circe for an entire year.

Odysseus's journey from Troy to Ithaca was filled with challenges. Polyphemus and Circe were just two of many meetings with monsters, friends, and enemies. It would take Odysseus 10 years before he finally arrived home.

1 *LEAVING TROY*

Once the Greeks had won the Trojan War, Odysseus set sail for home with 12 full ships.

6 *LAND OF THE LAESTRYGONIANS*

Next, the crew encountered the Laestrygonians—human-eating giants. The giants destroyed 11 of Odysseus's 12 ships.

7 *CIRCE'S SPELL*

With just one ship remaining, the men landed on Aeaea. There, they met the witch Circe, who turned some of them into pigs, then back into men.

8 *LAND OF THE DEAD*

Odysseus traveled to the entrance of the underworld to talk to the dead prophet Tiresias. He told Odysseus that Odysseus's wife, Penelope, was in trouble and he should hurry home.

11 *HELIOS'S CATTLE*

On the island of Thrinacia, Odysseus's men slaughtered the sacred cattle of Helios for a sacrifice. For this, they were punished by the gods—a storm destroyed their last ship and only Odysseus survived.

12 *CALYPSO*

The nymph Calypso rescued Odysseus after the storm, but refused to let him leave her for seven years because she wanted to marry him. Odysseus had to beg Athena to force the nymph to let him go.

3 THE LOTUS-EATERS

On the island of the lotus-eaters, a few men ate some of the local lotus fruit. They became addicted to it and refused to leave, so the rest of the crew had to go on without them.

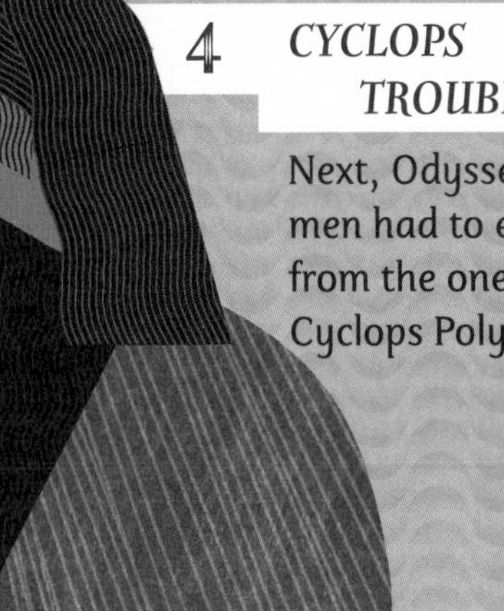

4 CYCLOPS TROUBLE

Next, Odysseus and his men had to escape from the one-eyed Cyclops Polyphemus.

2 LAND OF THE CICONES

First, the crew invaded the home of the Cicones, allies of the Trojans. However, they could not compete with the Ciconian army and fled.

5 AEOLUS'S GIFT

Aeolus, god of wind, gave Odysseus a bag of wind that would blow his ships home. However, his men, believing the bag contained treasure, opened it and the wind escaped.

9 SIRENS' SONG

The sirens were birds with the heads of women, whose song made sailors crash their ships. When they passed the sirens, Odysseus's crew stuffed their ears with beeswax to block out the beautiful but deadly music.

10 SCYLLA AND CHARYBDIS

Odysseus's ship had to sail through a channel guarded by the many-headed monster Scylla and the whirlpool Charybdis. They evaded Charybdis, but Scylla ate six of Odysseus's men.

13 LAND OF THE PHAEACIANS

Alone, Odysseus washed up on the shores of Phaeacia, where he met the princess Nausicaä. She sent him to the king and queen, who offered to help him. They gave him passage on one of their ships back to Ithaca.

14 ITHACA

When Odysseus finally reached Ithaca, he found that all was not well…

When Odysseus left for the war, his wife Penelope had taken over running the kingdom. When he didn't return from Troy for seven years, the kings from nearby lands assumed he was dead and they came to beg Penelope to marry them.

Penelope believed that Odysseus was still alive, though, and she made a plan to delay the suitors. She gathered them in a room and said, "I will choose a new husband, but only once I have woven a shroud for Odysseus's father, Laertes, who is growing old. Once it is finished, I will marry again."

The shroud was a special cloth used to bury the dead. Ordinarily, this task would not take long, but although Penelope spent every day weaving in front of the eager suitors, at night she would sneak back and undo all of her work.

In this way, Penelope managed to fool the suitors for three full years.

When Odysseus finally landed on the shores of Ithaca, he was alone, as he had lost every member of his crew on his travels. Waiting for him on the beach was the goddess Athena, who wanted to help him. "What has become of my kingdom?" he asked, and Athena told him about the suitors in his palace.

Odysseus was furious. "Do not worry," Athena said, "I have a plan." Using her powers, Athena disguised Odysseus as a beggar, so that no one would recognize him.

When Odysseus arrived at the palace claiming he had information about their king, no one suspected a thing. Queen Penelope came to hear what he knew. The disguised Odysseus said, "I met your husband on my travels. You should not worry, because he will be home very soon."

Penelope burst into tears.

"The suitors will not wait any longer," she said. "I've been forced to organize a competition to decide whom I will marry. Each suitor must try to string Odysseus's own bow, and I will wed the one who manages it."

"Do not worry," Odysseus the beggar replied, "your true husband will be there to win the contest himself."

The next day, the suitors gathered in the hall of the palace for the competition. One by one, they attempted to string the bow, but all failed. They laughed when a beggar picked up the bow, but he strung it in one swift movement.

The suitors suddenly realized who the beggar was, but Odysseus wanted revenge. He turned the bow on the suitors, firing arrow after arrow until they were all dead. Victorious, Odysseus then sent for Peneleope, and when she entered the hall she finally recognized her husband. She ran to him, overwhelmed by his return. Athena's spell lifted and before her stood the man she had missed for 20 years.

Odysseus and Penelope were finally reunited.

The Adventures of Atalanta

Atalanta was the daughter of King Iasos of Arcadia. Before her birth, her father had prayed to the gods that he would be blessed with a son.

When his wife gave birth to a daughter, Iasos was furious and abandoned the baby in the wilderness. The wailing Atalanta was discovered by a giant brown bear, but instead of attacking, the mother bear began to care for the human child.

The bear looked after Atalanta for many years and raised her in the wild.

As Atalanta grew into a woman, she proved to be a more skillful hunter and faster runner than anyone in all of Greece. Her fame spread, and she was approached by the hero Meleager. "Will you join my band of hunters and help us kill the Calydonian boar?" he asked. Atalanta readily agreed.

This boar was larger and more fearsome than any other, with tusks longer than those of an elephant. It had been sent by the goddess Artemis as a curse on Meleager's father, the king of Calydon, who had angered her. It was Meleager's duty as prince to catch the beast to protect his people.

The rest of the men laughed at the prince for inviting Atalanta, a woman, to join their hunt. “What help could she be?” they asked. However, Atalanta did not let their words upset her. She went with them through the forest, following the trail of broken trees pushed aside by the gigantic boar.

The men ignored her as they trekked through the forest, but Atalanta didn’t care.

When they caught up with the creature, the men ran toward it, weapons raised. One of them, Telamon, tripped on a tree root in his haste and tumbled to the ground. THUD! The boar turned its attention his way and prepared to charge. Quick-thinking Atalanta drew an arrow and fired at the beast. Her aim was true—the arrow hit the boar squarely in its chest and it staggered to a halt. Telamon was able to climb to his feet, and the other hunters sprang into action. Together, they soon defeated the boar. The people of Calydon were safe again and Atalanta was celebrated as a heroic huntress.

Atalanta took aim at the Calydonian boar.

Soon, Atalanta's name was known all over Greece. When her father discovered that she was alive, he was filled with guilt. Iasos looked for Atalanta so he could apologize for rejecting her as a baby. "Dearest daughter, can you ever forgive me?" he asked her. "Please return to Arcadia with me." Never having known a family before, Atalanta agreed.

When they arrived, she discovered that as a princess she was expected to marry and form an alliance to help her father's kingdom. Atalanta had traveled the world and achieved so much though, and she would only marry someone worthy of her. "I won't let you marry me off just for wealth and power," she told her father. "To prove themselves, my suitors will have to beat me at a trial."

Crowds came to cheer on the runners.

Atalanta decided that any man who wished to marry her had to demonstrate that he was as fast, if not faster, than she was, by challenging each of them in turn to a race. Those who were arrogant enough to go up against her but could not outrun her on the track would sacrifice their life.

Once again, the men of Greece laughed at her for thinking that a woman could beat a man, but one by one her potential husbands lost their races—and their lives. That is, until the hero Hippomenes took on her challenge.

Hippomenes was favored by the goddess Aphrodite, and she had given him three golden apples. He hid them in his clothes and asked to race Atalanta. She agreed. They lined up at the start, then they were off! Atalanta quickly took the lead, but Hippomenes took the first of the apples and threw it so that it rolled on the ground in front of her. Entranced by the golden fruit, she paused to pick it up. Continuing to run, he threw the second shining apple, and again she stopped to retrieve it. Hippomenes drew level with her.

Hippomenes overtook Atalanta and won the race.

Then came the final apple. Hippomenes dropped it at Atalanta's feet, and this time he was able to run past her and cross the finish line. Atalanta was annoyed at his trick, but he had won the race—and her hand in marriage.

ABOUT
THE
MYTHS

Today, thousands of years later, the Greek myths live on. This would never have been possible without the actions of the ancient Greeks themselves.

They passed down the tales of great adventures and tragic disasters from one generation to the next, for people to remember and enjoy. Importantly for us, they also recorded the details of the stories in solid objects we can study today, from scrolls of poetry to painted pottery.

WRITING

A lot of our knowledge of the myths comes from plays and poetry written down by authors in ancient Greece. The epic poems of ancient Greece are very long and tell the stories of gods and heroes.

The poet Homer wrote *The Iliad* and *The Odyssey*, two epic poems that tell the story of the Trojan War and Odysseus's adventures on his way home from Troy.

Plays were very popular in ancient Greece, and Euripides was a famous playwright. He wrote a play called *Medea* about Medea and her husband, the hero Jason.

Hesiod was a poet who wrote *The Theogony*, which explains the different generations of gods and how they were created, from Gaia to Zeus.

Friezes were long, stone wall-carvings showing scenes from myths and ancient Greek religious festivals. Many are found in the ruins of temples.

ART

Ancient Greek artists loved to tell the stories of the myths in their work. People could see these images from the myths every day, in all areas of their lives, on everything from vases to temples. Characters were also painted or carved out of stone.

STORYTELLING

One of the main ways that the myths were shared was by storytelling. Not everyone could read, so people would learn the myths by listening to older storytellers, who had memorized them. In this way, the myths were passed down from generation to generation.

Statues of mythological figures were made from stone or bronze. They were originally painted in bright colors when they were made, but the paint has worn away over time.

Painted pots, known as vases, allowed the ancient Greeks to have pictures from the myths in their own homes.

GREEK STORYTELLING

The ancient Greeks believed the myths were the true history of ancient Greece. Religion was a big part of everyday life and the stories of the myths were told in a variety of different ways. We know about the myths today because of ancient Greek writing and art.

GREEK VASES

The ancient Greeks used pots, which we call vases, to store grain, wine, oil, and many other things. Some were like bowls and others like cups, jugs, or jars. Vases were made from clay and were often painted with popular myths to entertain their owner or honor a particular god.

HERMES

A lekythos was a pitcher used for serving olive oil. This one was painted by an artist known as the Tithonos Painter in 470 BCE. It shows the messenger god, Hermes—recognizable by his winged shoes.

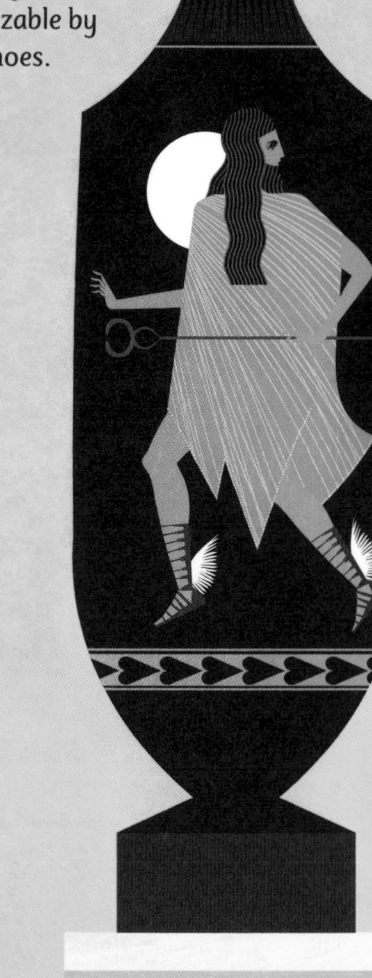

HERACLES BATTLES GERYON

This amphora from 540 BCE would have been used to store large amounts of grain or oil. It shows Heracles battling the three-headed giant Geryon during his tenth task.

VASE SHAPES

Ancient Greek vases came in all shapes and sizes. Some had lids and others were open, but they all had a specific purpose in ancient Greek life.

Kylix
Wine cup

Kantharos
Wine cup

Aryballos
Oil jar

Amphora
Oil, grain, or wine jar

ODYSSEUS AND THE SIRENS

A stamnos was used for storage or to mix wine and water. This one was painted by an artist known as the Siren Painter in 470 BCE. The artist is named after the image on the vase, which shows Odysseus trying to resist the song of the sirens.

ACHILLES KILLS PENTHESILEA

This amphora was painted by a man named Exekias in 525 BCE. It shows Achilles killing the Amazon Queen Penthesilea, who fought on the side of the Trojans during the Trojan War.

Stamnos
Oil, grain, or wine jar

Oinochoe
Wine pitcher

Krater
Mixing jar

Hydria
Water jar

Lekythos
Oil pitcher

TITANS

The Titans were an older generation of gods who gave birth to the Olympians, but were later overthrown by them during the War of the Titans. The Titans were the children of Gaia and Ouranos.

HORSES

Winged horses were used by the gods to pull their chariots through the sky. Pegasus was the most famous winged horse. He was born from the blood of Medusa when Perseus cut off her head.

GODS AND GODDESSES

The ancient Greeks worshiped various gods and goddesses. The 12 Olympians were the most powerful, but there were hundreds of other gods who were responsible for every part of life, from childbirth to rainbows.

CYCLOPES

The Cyclopes were one-eyed giants who were master craftsmen. They served as Hephaestus's assistants and made Zeus's thunderbolts. Some Cyclopes, such as Polyphemus, lived on Earth.

MYTHICAL BEINGS

Ancient Greek myths are filled with all sorts of fantastical beings. In addition to all-powerful gods, there are giants, magical creatures, and part-human, part-animal beasts. Many of these beings interfered with the lives of mortals, both helping and hurting them.

CENTAURS

Centaurs were men with the body of a horse from the waist down. Chiron was a famous centaur who helped many heroes on their adventures.

NYMPHS

These were divine spirits who took care of different parts of nature. They were always female, and different types were associated with different natural features, such as forests, mountains, rivers, or the sea.

HECATONCHEIRES

There were three Hecatoncheires—enormous giants with 50 heads and 100 hands each. Along with the Titans and the Cyclopes, they were children of Gaia and Ouranos.

SATYRS

Satyrs were nature spirits with the body and head of a man and the horns and legs of a goat. They worshiped the wine god Dionysus and were often shown playing pipes and drinking wine.

MONSTERS OF MYTH

Monsters from ancient Greek myths were terrifying beasts that tormented or killed mortals. Some were fearsome animals and others were part-human creatures, but all were frightful!

SIRENS

These were winged women who lived in caves along the coast. They would sing beautiful songs to try and make sailors crash their ships on the rocks.

DOGS

Lots of gods and heroes kept dogs. They weren't all ordinary pets, though. Cerberus, Hades' dog, and Cerberus's brother, Orthrus, had multiple heads and dragonlike tails.

THE HYDRA

The hydra was a huge monster that lived on the outskirts of Lerna. It had many heads on long, scaly necks, and if one head was chopped off, two more would grow back in its place.

THE CHIMAERA

This was a horrible monster that had the body of a lion, the head of a fire-breathing goat on its back, and a tail that ended in a dragon's head.

HARPIES

Harpies resembled giant birds, with their long, dangerous claws, but they had the heads of women. The gods sometimes sent them to punish mortals.

GIANTS

Giants often looked similar to humans, except that they were much, much larger. Some were so strong that they even fought the Olympian gods.

GORGONS

Gorgons, such as Medusa, were fearsome women whose stare turned mortals to stone. They had large wings, sharp claws, and snakes for hair.

DRAGONS

Dragons came in many shapes and sizes in ancient Greek mythology. Some were part-human, while others were huge serpents. Ancient Greek dragons did not usually have wings, but, rather, long scaly bodies.

SEA MONSTERS

The sea was full of monsters in Greek mythology, such as Ketos, a giant serpent. They served gods, such as Poseidon, and guarded the oceans.

THE MINOTAUR

The Minotaur was half-man, half-bull and ate human sacrifices. King Minos kept it trapped in the Labyrinth on the island of Crete.

NAMED FOR THE MYTHS

Mythology is all around us. Lots of things in the natural world are named after gods and creatures from ancient Greek myths. Many share characteristics with whomever or whatever they are named after.

PLANETS

Most of the planets in our solar system are named after ancient Greek gods. They have been given the Latin versions, used by the ancient Romans, of their original Greek names. The Romans admired the ancient Greeks and shared many of their gods.

Venus (Aphrodite) is named after the goddess of love. It is the brightest planet in the sky.

Earth (Gaia) is the only planet not named for a god, although the goddess Gaia is often known as Mother Earth.

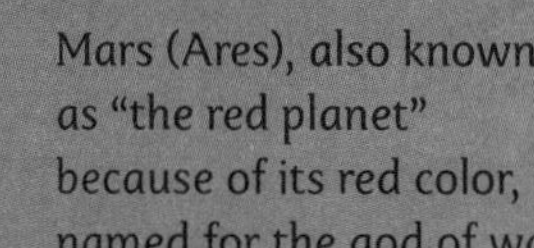

Mars (Ares), also known as "the red planet" because of its red color, is named for the god of war.

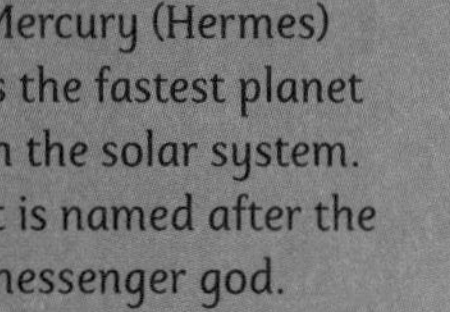

Mercury (Hermes) is the fastest planet in the solar system. It is named after the messenger god.

ANIMALS

Lots of animals have names that come from Greek mythology because people thought their behavior or appearance was similar to characters from myth.

The harpy eagle has the scientific name *Harpia harpyja*. It is named after the mythological harpy, which had the body of a bird and the face of a woman.

The golden myotis bat has the scientific name *Myotis midastactus*. It gets its name from King Midas because of its golden-yellow fur. The translation of the Latin *midastactus* is "Midas touch."

Crocus was a mortal who fell in love with a nymph named Smilax. She didn't return his love, however, and the gods transformed the heartbroken Crocus into a crocus flower.

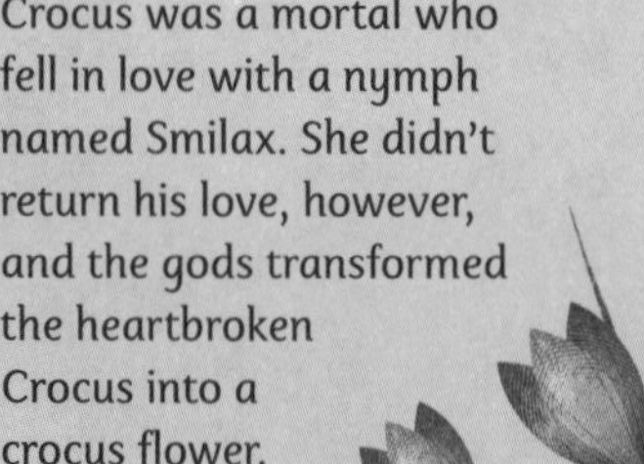

Hyacinths are named for a mortal friend of the god Apollo, Hyacinthus, whom Apollo accidentally killed. Where Hyacinthus fell, the flower bloomed.

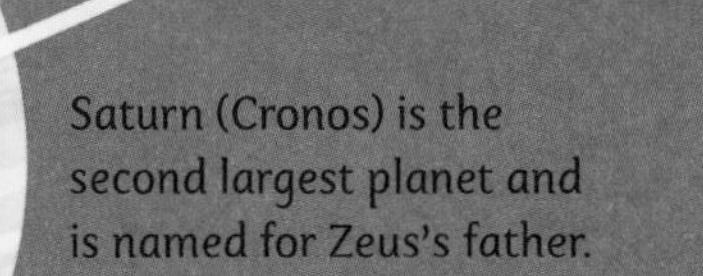

Saturn (Cronos) is the second largest planet and is named for Zeus's father.

Uranus (Ouranos) is named for Gaia's husband and Zeus's grandfather—the first god to rule over the heavens.

Jupiter (Zeus) is the largest planet in the solar system and takes its name from the king of the gods.

Neptune (Poseidon) is a blue planet named for the god of the sea.

CONSTELLATIONS

Different constellations of stars are named after different characters from ancient mythology, based on the shape they make in the sky. Some were named by the ancient Greeks themselves.

The constellation Heracles shows the hero with a club in his hand.

Centaurus is named after the first-ever centaur—a mythical creature that was half-man, half-horse.

Sisyphus is a group of dung beetles that rolls balls of dung. The beetles are named for Sisyphus, a mortal whose punishment in the underworld was to continuously roll a boulder up a hill.

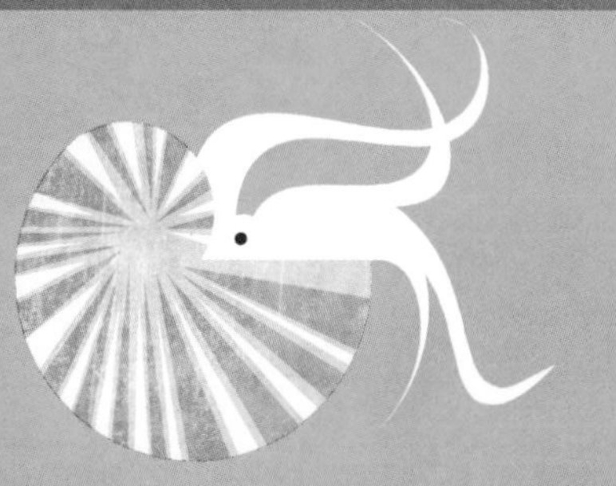

Argonauts are a type of octopus that make a thin shell. They are named after the Argonauts, Jason's crew who sailed the Argo.

The little owl was a symbol of the goddess Athena. The little owl's scientific name is *Athene noctua*.

Proteas get their name from Proteus, a child of Poseidon who could shape-shift. This is because their flowers come in so many different colors and shapes.

PLANTS

Many botanists named the plants they found after characters and creatures in ancient Greek mythology. Some plants are named directly for their part in certain myths.

WORSHIPING THE GODS

Religion was a huge part of every ancient Greek's life. People had small shrines at home where they would worship the gods and offer sacrifices, but they also took part in large public celebrations. Athletic games and festivals in sacred places were common and often dedicated to specific gods.

FESTIVALS AND GAMES

Festivals and athletic games were held in honor of the gods. Festivals often involved dancing, sacrifices, and theater. Big athletic games were held regularly, such as the Olympic Games held every four years. Winners were awarded wreaths—crowns made from leaves.

The Pythian Games were held in honor of Apollo, and athletes could win a laurel wreath.

The Olympic Games were held in honor of Zeus, and the winners received a wreath of olive leaves.

The Nemean Games were also held in honor of Zeus, but the champions were given a celery wreath.

The Isthmian Games were held in honor of Poseidon. Each victorious athlete won a celery or pine wreath.

SACRED PLACES

There were lots of different kinds of sacred places all over Greece. Certain towns or islands were associated with a particular god or goddess.

Delphi was where the famous priestess of Apollo, the Pythia, lived. People would visit her to hear the future.

A secret festival dedicated to Demeter and Persephone was held in the town of Eleusis.

TEMPLES

The ancient Greeks built temples to honor different gods. People would go there to leave gifts, such as small statues, which would be looked after by priests and priestesses. Some temples contained a giant statue of a god or goddess.

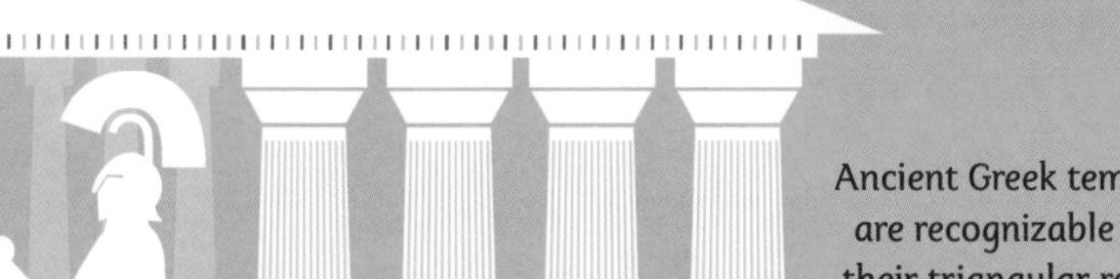

Ancient Greek temples are recognizable by their triangular roof, supported by rows of columns.

The town of Olympia had many temples, but the biggest was the Temple of Zeus. The Olympic Games were held here in his honor.

The island of Delos was sacred to Apollo and had a temple that contained a giant statue of the god.

SACRIFICES

Sacrifices were gifts offered to the gods to gain their favor. Some were personal gifts at home, others were big community offerings. Food and drink were popular choices, and these were often burned.

Wine was a common drink in ancient Greece. People would pour out some wine for the gods before every meal.

Animals, such as sheep and cows, were popular sacrifices. They were killed and certain parts were burned, while the meat was given to worshipers.

MOUNT OLYMPUS

Mount Olympus is a real mountain in Greece. The top is so tall that it can't be seen from below, and the ancient Greeks believed this was where the main gods lived. These gods were known as the Olympians, after the home they shared. Historians usually count 12 Olympians, but this doesn't always include the same gods.

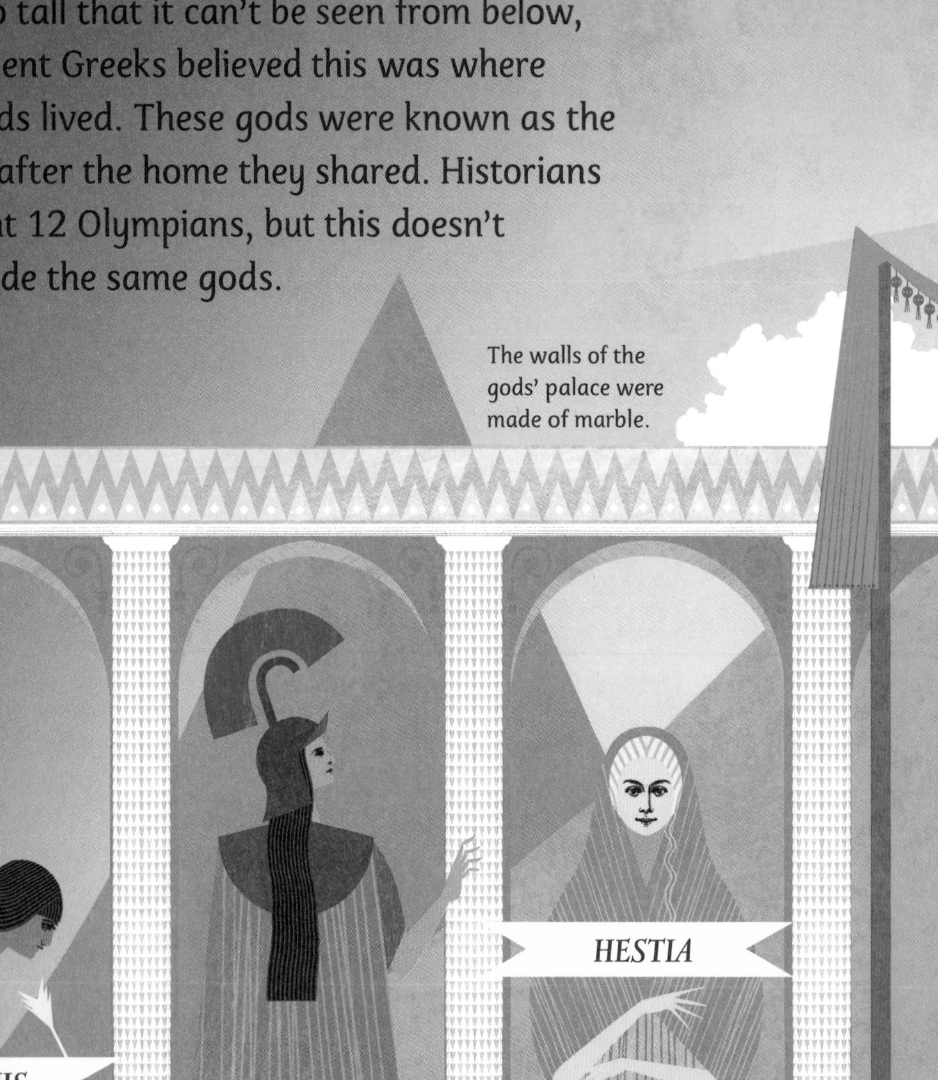

Mount Olympus is the tallest mountain in all of Greece.

The walls of the gods' palace were made of marble.

A sacred flame was kept burning on Mount Olympus at all times.

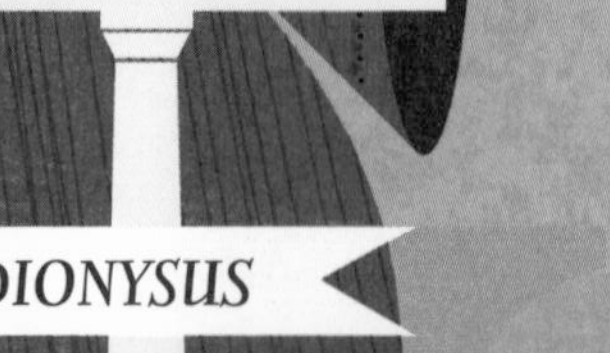

AMBROSIA AND NECTAR

The gods ate ambrosia and drank sweet-smelling nectar instead of mortal food and drink. If a mortal ate ambrosia, they would become a god themselves.

PALACE IN THE SKY

The gods lived in a palace made from marble and bronze surrounded by golden pavements. The palace sat above the clouds so humans could not see it.

GATES TO OLYMPUS

Olympus had strong walls to protect it from attack. The only way in and out was through a pair of golden gates that were always fiercely guarded.

ZEUS

APOLLO

HERMES

ARES

TWELVE OLYMPIANS

These were the 12 most powerful gods. Hades was sometimes left out, because he lived in the underworld, as was Dionysus, because he was younger than the other Olympians.

APHRODITE

POSEIDON

HEPHAESTUS

DEMETER

ASPHODEL FIELDS

The underworld was carpeted with large fields of asphodel—a type of plant with pale white flowers. This plant was the only food that souls could eat.

JUDGMENT

Minos, Rhadamanthus, and Aeacus were responsible for judging souls who entered the underworld. They had once been mortal men but were granted this honor by the gods.

GATES TO THE UNDERWORLD

The underworld was protected by huge metal gates that were guarded by the three-headed dog Cerberus. These gates stopped the souls of the dead from escaping.

THE FURIES

The Furies were three goddesses responsible for punishing people who committed evil acts by driving them insane, both in the land of the living and the dead.

The Furies had large wings that carried them as fast as the wind.

TARTARUS

Tartarus was the deepest, darkest part of the underworld, where Zeus had imprisoned the Titans who had fought against him. It was also where souls were punished for doing wrong in their lives, such as Tantalus, Sisyphus, and the Danaïdes.

Tantalus's punishment was to stand forever between water and a fruit tree, but never to be able to eat or drink.

ACHERON RIVER

In order to get to the underworld souls had to cross the Acheron River. They had to pay the ferryman, Charon, one coin to board his boat. If a body hadn't been given a coin in the land of the living, then they would be stuck by the river forever.

THE UNDERWORLD

The underworld was where a mortal's soul traveled to after death. Here, they would spend the rest of eternity. It was a dark place, and once they were there, no one could return to the world above. It was ruled by the god Hades with the help of his wife, Persephone.

ELYSIUM

Elysium was an island in the underworld reserved for important heroes, such as Orpheus, who had been honored by the gods.

The three fates were named Klotho, Lachesis, and Atropos.

Sisyphus was sentenced to roll a rock up a hill, but just before he got to the top, it always rolled down again.

THE FATES

The Fates were the three goddesses of destiny. They used their spinning wheel to spin threads that represented mortal lives and cut them when each life came to an end.

The Danaïdes were sisters cursed to try and use jugs to fill a leaking bathtub for eternity.

PALACE OF HADES AND PERSEPHONE

Hades and Persephone lived in a private palace made entirely of gold. From here, they ruled the rest of the underworld.

Charon was the ferryman who brought souls to the underworld.

PRONUNCIATION GUIDE

ACASTOS
a-KASS-toss

ACHERON
A-ker-on

ACHILLES
a-KILL-eez

ACRISIOS
a-KRISS-ee-os

AEACUS
EE-a-kuss

AEAEA
ee-EY-a

AEËTES
ai-EY-teez

AEGEUS
ee-JEE-uss

AEGIS
EE-jiss

AEOLUS
ee-OH-luss

AETHER
EETH-er

AETHIOPIA
eeth-ee-OH-pee-a

AGAMEMNON
a-ga-MEM-non

ALCMENE
alk-MEE-nee

ALECTO
a-LEK-toh

AMBROSIA
am-BRO-zhee-a

AMPHITRITE
am-fi-TRI-tee

ANDROMEDA
an-DRA-me-da

ANTIGONE
an-TI-goh-nee

APHRODITE
aff-roh-DAI-tee

APOLLO
a-PA-loh

ARACHNE
a-RAK-nee

ARCADIA
ah-KAY-dee-a

ARES
EHR-eez

ARIADNE
a-ree-AD-nee

ARGONAUT
AR-ge-not

ARGOS
AR-goss

ARTEMIS
AR-te-miss

ASPHODEL
ASS-fe-dell

ATALANTA
at-a-LAN-ta

ATHENA
ath-EE-na

ATHENS
A-thens

ATLANTIAN
at-LAN-tee-an

ATLAS
AT-les

ATROPOS
A-tro-puss

AUGEUS
ow-JEE-uss

BELLEROPHON
beh-LER-eh-fun

BRISEIS
bree-SAY-eez

CADMUS
KAD-muss

CADUCEUS
ka-DOO-see-us

CALYDON
KA-li-don

CALYDONIAN
KA-li-doh-nee-an

CALYPSO
ka-LIP-so

CASSIOPEIA
kass-ee-oh-PEE-a

CENTAUR
SEN-tor

CEPHEUS
SEE-fee-uss

CERBERUS
SER-ber-uss

CHAOS
KAY-oss

CHARON
KAH-ron

CHARYBDIS
ka-RIB-diss

CHIMAERA
kai-MEER-a

CHIRON
KAI-ron

CICONES
KAI-koh-nees

CIRCE
SER-see

COLCHIS
KAL-kiss

CORINTH
KOR-inth

CREON
KREE-on

CRETAN
KREE-tan

CRETE
KREET

CRONUS
KROH-nuss

CYCLOPES
SAI-klo-pees

CYCLOPS
SAI-klops

DAEDALUS
DED-a-luss

DANAË
da-NA-ee

DANAÏDES
da-NAI-a-deez

DEIPHOBUS
DEA-foh-buss

DELOS
DEE-loss

DELPHI
DEL-fi

DEMETER
deh-MEE-ter

DEUCALION
dew-KAL-ee-on

DICTYS
DIK-tees

DIOMEDES
dai-a-MEE-deez

DIONYSUS
dai-a-NAI-suss

ELEUSINIAN
el-yoo-SIN-ee-an

ELYSIUM
eh-LI-zee-um

EOS
ee-OSS

EPEIOS
eh-PEE-oss

EPIMETHEUS
eh-pee-MEE-thee-uss

EREBUS
EHR-eh-buss

ERIS
EHR-iss

EROS
EER-oss

ERYMANTHIAN
eh-ri-MAN-thee-an

ETNA
ET-na

EURIPIDES
yoo-RIP-ih-deez

EUROPA
yoo-ROH-pa

EURYALE
yoo-RAI-al-ee

EURYDICE
yoo-RID-i-see

EURYSTHEUS
yoo-RISS-thee-uss

EXEKIAS
ex-EH-kee-ass

GAIA
GUY-a

GERYON
GEH-ree-on

GORGON
GOR-gen

HADES
HEY-deez

HECATONCHEIRES
hek-ah-ton-KI-reys

HECTOR
HEK-tor

HELIOS
HEE-lee-oss

HEMERA
HEH-meh-ra

HEPHAESTUS
heh-FE-stuss

HERA
HEER-a

HERACLES
HEH-ra-kleez

HERMES
HER-meez

HESIOD
HEH-see-od

HESPERIDES
hess-PEH-ri-deez

HESTIA
HESS-tee-a

HIPPOLYTA
hi-POL-i-ta

HIPPOMENES
hi-POH-mee-neez

HOMER
HOH-mer

HYACINTHUS
hai-a-SIN-thuss

HYDRA
HAI-dra

IASOS
AI-a-soss

ICARIA
i-KAR-ee-a

ICARUS
IK-a-russ

IO
AI-oh

IOBATES
ai-oh-BAT-eez

IOLAOS
AI-oh-lass

IOLCHOS
EE-ol-koss

ISTHMIAN
ISSTH-mee-an

ITHACA
ITH-a-ka

KAMPE
KAM-pee

KETOS
KEE-toss

KLOTHO
KLOH-thoh

LACHESIS
LAK-eh-siss

LAERTES
ley-ER-teez

LAESTRYGONIAN
les-try-GOH-nee-an

LEMNOS
lem-NOSS

LERNA
LER-na

LETO
LEE-toh

LYDIAN
LID-ee-an

LYCIA
LI-see-a

MAENAD
MEE-nad

MAIA
MAI-a

MEDEA
meh-DEE-a

MEDUSA
meh-DOO-sah

MEGAERA
meg-AI-ra

MEGARA
MEH-ga-ra

MELEAGER
mell-EE-ey-ger

MENELAUS
men-eh-LEY-uss

METIS
MEH-tiss

MIDAS
MAI-dass

MINOS
MAI-nuss

MINOTAUR
MAI-nuh-tor

MYCENAE
MAI-see-nee

MYRINA
mi-REE-na

NAUSICAÄ
NAW-si-kia

NAXOS
NAK-soss

NEMEAN
neh-MEE-an

NYMPH
NIMF

NYX
NIKS

OCEANUS
oh-see-AH-nuss

ODYSSEUS
oh-DIS-see-uss

OLYMPIA
oh-LIMP-ee-a

OLYMPIAN
oh-LIMP-ee-an

OLYMPUS
oh-LIMP-uss

ORION
oh-RAI-on

ORPHEUS
OR-fee-uss

ORTHRUS
OR-thrus

OURANOS
OO-ran-oss

PANDORA
pan-DOR-a

PARIS
PA-riss

PATROCLUS
pa-TROK-luss

PEGASUS
PEH-ga-siss

PELEUS
PEH-lee-uss

PELIAS
PEE-lee-ass

PENELOPE
peh-NELL-oh-pee

PENTHESILEA
penth-ess-i-LEY-a

PERSEPHONE
per-SEF-oh-nee

PERSEUS
PER-see-uss

PHAEACIA
fee-EY-sha

PHAËTHON
FEY-a-ton

PHILONOE
FIL-oh-NOH-ee

PHINEUS
FIN-ee-uss

PHOENICIA
fi-NI-she-a

PHRYGIA
fri-JEE-a

PLEIONE
PLEE-oh-nee

POLYDECTES
poli-DEK-tees

POLYPHEMUS
poll-a-FEE-muss

POSEIDON
poh-SAI-don

PRIAM
PRAI-am

PROMETHEUS
pro-MEE-thee-uss

PROTEUS
PROH-tee-uss

PSYCHE
SAI-kee

PYRRHA
PI-ra

PYTHIA
PITH-ee-ah

RHADAMANTHUS
rad-a-MAN-thuss

RHEA
REE-a

SATYR
SAY-ter

SCYLLA
SILL-a

SELENE
seh-LEE-nee

SEMELE
SEH-meh-lee

SERIPHOS
SER-ih-foss

SICILY
SISS-i-lee

SILENUS
sai-LEEN-uss

SINTIAN
SIN-tee-an

SIREN
SAI-ren

SISYPHUS
SISS-i-fuss

SMILAX
SMAI-laks

SPARTA
SPAR-ta

STYMPHALIAN
stim-FAH-lee-an

SYMPLEGADES
sim-PLEH-gah-deez

STYX
STIKS

TALARIA
ta-LAI-ree-a

TANTALUS
TAN-ta-luss

TARTARUS
TAR-ta-russ

TELAMON
TEH-la-mon

THEBES
THEEBS

THESEUS
THEE-see-uss

THESSALY
THEH-sa-lee

THETIS
THEH-tiss

THRACE
THREYSS

THRINACIA
thrin-AH-kee-a

TIRESIAS
tai-REE-see-ass

TISIPHONE
ti-SI-foh-nee

TITAN
TIE-tan

TITHONOS
ti-THO-noss

TRITON
TRAI-ton

TROJAN
TROH-jan

TROY
TROI

TYPHOEUS
TAI-fee-uss

ZEUS
ZOOSS

GLOSSARY

ACHERON RIVER river in the underworld. Souls can only cross it in the boat of the ferryman, Charon

AMAZONS group of warrior women who live apart from the rest of society

AMBROSIA food of the gods that can make mortals immortal if they eat it

APHRODITE goddess of love and beauty and one of the 12 Olympians

APOLLO god of music and one of the 12 Olympians

ARES god of war and one of the 12 Olympians

ARTEMIS goddess of hunting and one of the 12 Olympians

ASPHODEL FIELDS part of the underworld covered in fields of white asphodel flowers

ATHENA goddess of war and wisdom and one of the 12 Olympians

CENTAUR creature with the head and torso of a man and the body of a horse

CERBERUS Hades' pet dog who has three heads and guards the gates to the underworld

CHARIOT small roofless carriage pulled by horses

CHIMAERA monster that looks like a lion, but with a dragon's head for a tail and a fire-breathing goat's head poking out of its back

CITY-STATE independent city, and sometimes the surrounding area, that rules itself and has its own king or government

CONSTELLATION collection of stars in the sky that make a shape

CYCLOPS one-eyed giant. Three brother Cyclopes make Zeus's thunderbolts

DEMETER goddess of the harvest and one of the 12 Olympians

DIONYSUS god of wine, parties, and theater. He is sometimes counted as one of the 12 Olympians

ELYSIUM island in the underworld reserved for people the gods want to honor

EPIC POEM long poem that tells a story, usually a myth, such as *The Iliad*, which is about the Trojan War

FATES three goddesses who decide the lifespan of mortals

FURIES three goddesses who punish wrongdoers

GAIA goddess of the Earth. She was the first god to appear

GAMES athletic event held throughout ancient Greece in honor of the gods. Events include running and chariot racing

GOD powerful immortal being. Each god is in charge of a different part of the world and may even be that part of the world—for example, the goddess Gaia is also the Earth

GORGON monstrous woman with snakes for hair who can turn mortals to stone by looking at them

HADES god of the underworld who rules over the souls of the dead. He is sometimes counted as one of the 12 Olympians

HARPY creature that is half-bird, half-woman

HECATONCHEIRES giants with 50 heads and 100 arms each

HEPHAESTUS god of smiths and volcanoes and one of the 12 Olympians

HERA goddess of marriage and queen of the gods. She is married to Zeus

HERMES messenger god and one of the 12 Olympians

HESTIA goddess of the hearth and one of the 12 Olympians

HYDRA monster with multiple serpentlike heads. If one head is cut off, one or more grow back in its place

IMMORTAL being who will live forever and cannot be killed

KRONOS Titan and the father of Zeus. Also the god of time

LABYRINTH maze in which the Minotaur is imprisoned

LOOM device for weaving thread into cloth

LYRE musical instrument with a solid frame and strings that can be plucked

MAENAD woman who worships Dionysus through lively parties and dancing

MINOTAUR half-man, half-bull monster that eats humans and is trapped in the Labyrinth

MORTAL someone with no divine powers; an ordinary human

MOUNT ETNA volcano on the east coast of Sicily where Hephaestus was believed to do his work

MOUNT OLYMPUS tallest mountain in Greece and the home of the gods

NECTAR liquid drunk by the gods, supposedly sweeter than honey

NYMPH goddess in charge of part of the natural world. Nymphs are less powerful than the Olympians

OATH promise that cannot be broken. The gods swear oaths to Styx, who punishes them if the oath is broken

ORACLE place people go to find out their future or receive a message for their people

OURANOS god of the sky

PEGASUS flying horse born from the blood of Medusa

POSEIDON god of the sea and one of the 12 Olympians

PROPHECY message about the future sent down by the gods

PYTHIA powerful prophetess in ancient Greece and priestess of Apollo. She lives in Delphi

SACRIFICE gift given to the gods by mortals. Sacrifices can be objects, food, or drink and are often burned

SATYR half-goat, half-man creature who serves Dionysus

SHROUD cloth used to cover the body of a dead person

SICKLE curved metal knife

SIREN half-bird, half-woman monster that sings songs to lure sailors to their death

SMITH person who makes things out of metal

SOUL part of a mortal that lives on in the underworld after death

STYX RIVER river that separates the underworld from the land of the living. Gods swear oaths on this river

SUITOR man who wishes to marry a princess or queen

SYMPLEGADES pair of rocks out at sea that clash together and destroy ships

TAPESTRY type of artwork woven from thread

TARTARUS deepest part of the underworld where the Titans are imprisoned

THUNDERBOLT weapon used by Zeus. They are made for him by the Cyclopes

TITAN god who existed before Zeus and the other Olympians

TRIDENT three-pronged spear used by Poseidon as a weapon

UNDERWORLD where souls go after death. The underworld is ruled by Hades

VASE pot used by the ancient Greeks. Different shapes and sizes of vase are used for different purposes, such as storing olive oil

WITCH woman who practices magic and performs spells

ZEUS king of the gods and ruler of the world. He is married to Hera

INDEX

Written by Jean Menzies
Consultant Professor Edith Hall
Illustrated by Katie Ponder

Senior Commissioning Designer Joanne Clark
Project Editor Olivia Stanford
Editor Kathleen Teece
US Editor Margaret Parrish
US Senior Editor Shannon Beatty
Managing Editor Jonathan Melmoth
Managing Art Editor Diane Peyton Jones
Senior Pre-producer Nikoleta Parasaki
Producer Ena Matagic
Publishing Director Sarah Larter

First American Edition, 2020
Published in the United States by DK Publishing
1450 Broadway, Suite 801, New York, NY 10018

21 22 23 24 10 9 8 7 6 5 4 3 2
007–315516–July/2020

Published in Great Britain by Dorling Kindersley Limited.

A catalog record for this book is available from the Library of Congress.
ISBN 978-1-4654-9153-4

DK books are available at special discounts when purchased in bulk for sales promotions, premiums, fund-raising, or educational use.
For details, contact: DK Publishing Special Markets, 1450 Broadway, Suite 801, New York, NY 10018
SpecialSales@dk.com

Printed and bound in Canada

For the curious

www.dk.com

The publisher would like to thank the following people for their assistance in the preparation of this book: Katie Lawrence for editorial assistance; Simon Mumford for cartography; Caroline Hunt for proofreading; and Helen Peters for the index.

ABOUT THE AUTHOR

Jean Menzies runs a podcast about classics and mythology, and has a YouTube channel, where she discusses literature and history. She has spoken about ancient Greece to audiences of all ages, and is currently researching for a PhD in women in classical Athens.

ABOUT THE ILLUSTRATOR

Katie Ponder is an award-winning illustrator whose work has been featured in exhibitions at Somerset House, The Lyric Theatre, and Glyndebourne opera house. Her inspirations include the ballet, ghost stories, and the greenhouses at Kew Gardens.

MAIN SOURCES

- Apollodorus, *The Library of Greek Mythology*, translated by Robin Hard, Oxford University Press, Oxford, 2008
- Apollonius of Rhodes, *Jason and the Golden Fleece (The Argonautica)*, translated by Richard Hunter, Oxford University Press, Oxford, 2009
- Apuleius, *The Golden Ass*, translated by P. G. Walsh, Oxford University Press, Oxford, 2008
- Diodorus Siculus, *Library*, translated by C. H. Oldfather, Harvard University Press, Cambridge, 1989
- Hesiod, *Catalogue of Women*, translated by Glenn W. Most, Harvard University Press, Cambridge, 2007
- Hesiod, *Theogony & Works and Days*, translated by M. L. West, Oxford University Press, Oxford, 2008
- Homer, *The Iliad*, translated by Richmond Lattimore, University of Chicago Press, Chicago, 2011
- Homer, *The Odyssey*, translated by Emily Wilson, W. W. Norton & Company, London, 2017
- Hyginus, *Constellation Myths*, translated by Robin Hard, Oxford University Press, Oxford, 2015
- Ovid, *Metamorphosis*, translated by A. D. Melville, Oxford University Press, Oxford, 2008
- Pindar, *The Complete Odes*, translated by Anthony Verity, Oxford University Press, Oxford, 2008
- Various, *The Homeric Hymns*, translated by Michael Crudden, Oxford University Press, Oxford, 2008